Dead in Bed

"Reading *Dead in Bed*, the first twisty and fast-paced book in Rosen's new mystery series, The Senior Sleuths, I found myself laughing and biting my nails at the same time. What a ride!"

~ Claudia Riess, Author of *Semblance of Guilt* and *Love and Other Hazards*

Dead In Bed

A Senior Sleuths Mystery

by

M. Glenda Rosen

Copyright Page

Dead in Bed
A Senior Sleuths Mystery

First Edition | February 2018

Level Best Books
www.levelbestbooks.com

Trade Paperback ISBN- 978-1947915022
Also Available in e-book

Printed in the United States of America

To my family with much love.

And to David and Joyce for their amazing support.

Prologue

The Zimmermans

I'm Dora Zimmerman.

My husband is the handsome, irascible and incredibly charming Dick Zimmerman.

He does love to gamble.

We have an interesting, rather odd, group of friends and acquaintances including a bookie, a chief of police, a retired physician, a professional woman gambler, a rabbi, a medical examiner, the owner of a popular Manhattan bar, and a few other delightfully entertaining characters and connections including Frankie Socks, who we know for a fact was in the Witness Protection Program.

More on that later.

Dick and I have been married for forty years and he tells everyone he's retired. He used to be a criminal attorney. He defended a lot of good guys. He also defended some bad guys. They owe him big favors. He doesn't want them. Unless he needs them or they need him. It's a mutual professional relationship—of sorts.

I was a lawyer, then a judge in divorce court. Believe me, there were some criminals there worse than murderers. Men and women who abused or caused pain for their children or hid money so they wouldn't have to pay alimony or child support. They would sometimes fight in court. It was like being in a boxing ring and I was the referee. I delighted in giving the knockout punch to any man or woman who deserved it.

Dick and I have two grown sons. They love us and we love them.

They also think we're a little off our rockers because we seem to keep getting involved in chasing after criminals, especially murderers. We get wrapped up in helping solve crimes. Then, there is our strange group of friends.

We see our boys once in a while. They check on us, send us birthday and anniversary cards and pray we won't visit them for the holidays. They seem to fear we will bring a criminal element along with the pumpkin pie.

Possibly because we did a few times.

Oh well. As I said we love them and they love us. From a distance. We don't mind. We're having too much fun.

We have a penthouse condo in Skyline Vista in Manhattan, known as the Mansion, and another at Desert Vista in Las Vegas. We get to step out on our balconies and see great views. Sometimes we also see a crime happening or a suspect running away. Dick or I will text Frankie Socks hoping he can follow them. Then, the chase is on.

Socks joined us in Vegas once, but that's for another story.

We enjoy Broadway theatre and great restaurants in Manhattan. Dick and I love the beautiful fashions and wonderful places to shop in the city. Everyone is entitled to a few flaws, even us.

As for Vegas, of course there is great entertainment, dining, and gambling.

I certainly don't cook, but we delight in entertaining our friends with lavish parties of caviar, champagne and music. After all, what are friends for if not to spoil and enjoy them?

A few months ago, a medical examiner friend of mine suggested I write about our escapades. I thought, why not?

Let me tell you what happened.

It begins with a murder.

Of course.

Chapter 1

Dead in Bed

The alarm sent close to a hundred seniors into the halls and guest areas of Skyline Vista Condos dressed in their finest nightclothes.

Okay, some not so fine.

Dick and Dora Zimmerman, the Zimms, wore matching dark blue, satin pajamas with pale blue piping, and of course matching slippers. Everything was first class with them. Their clothes and fashion sense were impeccable, as if the fashion police watched them constantly. They had the money and the means to buy beautiful things and they simply figured, why not?

Zero, the resident bookie and one of the Zimms best friends, joined them. He wore his very own fine sleepwear—red sweatpants, white tennis socks and a dark grey t-shirt with the words *You bet Your a... I Can.*

The natives rumbled.

Annoyed, scared, concerned, annoyed, anxious, curious and, oh yeah, very annoyed.

"What's happening?"

"Why did the damn alarm go off?"

"Is there a fire?"

"Maybe a burglar?"

"Maybe a rapist?"

The last question came from eighty-nine-year-young Bertie Gladstone, who sounded more interested than concerned. Every day she put on makeup, fixed her bleached-blonde hair, and dressed up in colorful clothes and jewelry to match. Ready to face her public, off she went with her walker, a gift of having had a slight stroke a year earlier. In truth her best feature had always been and still was her sense of humor. She delighted in being playful.

Bertie was a big flirt.

When asked why she dressed so fancy every day, Bertie responded, "I'm looking for my fourth husband."

She meant it.

Very sound of mind, this little lady was aware that her youngest son, one of three children from her first husband, Carson Gladstone, a respected New York newspaper man, was also a compulsive gambler.

Zero and Dick were delighted to have him join their poker games when he could. They were equally delighted to take his money. He wasn't a very good poker player. But he did love the ponies. There too he lost more than he won.

The fuss in the hallway continued.

"When can I go back to my place?"

"I need my sleep."

"Are the police coming?"

The night manager, Vincent Blair, forty-something and quite a charmer with his shoulder-length dirty blond hair, was studying to be a nurse. At least that's what he told everyone.

The older women adored him. He knew how to charm them.

Maybe too much.

"Everything is fine," Vincent said, running his fingers through the front of his hair. "The alarm appears to have gone off accidently. There are no fires. No rapists. No robberies. No problems."

"Something set it off, Vincent."

"Where are the police?" shouted Zero.

"The police are on their way," Vincent said, giving him a dirty look. Like Zero really cared.

"If I don't get eight hours a sleep a night, I'm a wreck," one woman said, storming off to her own place.

"'Bitch' is more like it," replied the lady's long suffering husband.

Dora turned to Dick and Zero. "Doesn't sound right to me."

"I'm going back to bed," Dick said and off he went with that charming grin and sexy saunter that drove Bertie Gladstone and more than a few other ladies to distraction.

"Get rid of Dora and I'll be yours," she told him repeatedly.

Dick would laugh, give Bertie a kiss on her rouge-colored cheek and whisper, "Pretty soon, sweetheart."

Bertie would wink at him. They had been doing this routine for months.

"Zero, let's take a stroll around the joint." Putting her arm through his, Dora guided him away from the crowd and a very nervous acting Vincent.

It was easy to see the Zimms love each other. Their affection showed in how they treated each other with simple gestures others noticed, perhaps even wish they had in their own lives. It could be walking arm in arm up Fifth Avenue, respecting each other's points of view even if they differ, or laughing and smiling when in each other's company, even when it involved murder.

For some reason crime seemed to find them during their careers and afterwards. Old friends ask for help, new friends seek out their guidance, the police ask for their assistance and sometimes a murder just falls into their lap.

Then there were criminals who had attempted to shut them up on a number of occasions.

On top of a fireplace mantle, wherever they are living, two photos of them stand side-by-side. One is from when they first met, younger, more carefree looking. The second was taken when they recently celebrated their fortieth wedding anniversary.

Dick still handsome, with dark green eyes, his full head of hair, grey except for a few black streaks reminiscent of his youth, dressed in an Armani tuxedo.

Dora, elegant, attractive, refusing to cut her hair short, keeping it shoulder length, dark brown covering the grey, blue eyes, and thanks to her gene pool, still slender. In their anniversary photo she's wearing a smoky blue satin Vera Wang gown, the exact color of her eyes.

Like everyone their lives had their share of disappointments and hurts. They preferred not to talk about those. They were too grateful for the good in their lives. They developed a particular kind of resilience that had given them the audacity to continue their accomplishments in spite of any losses.

The center of their lives' work was justice.

Not something they could let go of even in their so-called retirement. Dora found solving crimes exciting and challenging. Dick would have preferred poker, ponies and partying. Somehow Dora always managed to push him into helping solve any crime that came their way.

He would say no, no way. She would give him a hug, a kiss on the cheek, put her arm through his, or any one of a number of ways she could charm him into saying maybe.

Then she had him. He knew that too.

Dick would catch Zero laughing at this exchange promising him, "Don't think you're not involved too."

It seemed murder frequently beckoned them.

Dora loved to play detective even though she had found herself in a few tight spots in the past. Like almost getting killed, nearly run over by a horse and carriage in Central Park and once hit on the head with a volume of Shakespeare.

"Ready, Lady D?"

Zero had known Dora since they went to high school together in Manhattan. He loved to call her Lady D after she played the role of a princess in a school play. They had a special connection—both being trouble makers while pretending innocence.

Over the years, they had many good laughs remembering the time they glued an apple on a teacher's desk, left a burner on in the chemistry lab setting off the school fire alarm and, of course, the time the principal couldn't find her car. Dora and Zero had let the air out of the tires and called a tow company to pick it up watching from behind the corner as it was driven away.

How they were never caught is still a mystery. Maybe because they always had a few other accomplices looking out for them. Like now.

Two young police officers walked in through the front door laughing and chatting, so Dora and Zero ducked down the long corridor on the first floor of the Mansion leading to the dining area, past the exercise room and toward the rear elevators.

"These are usually false alarms," they heard one of the officers say. "It happens several times a year. Someone sets it off by going out the door. The one with the big sign that says NO EXIT."

Young and cocky, they hadn't noticed someone hiding outside the front of the building. Someone who walked quickly uptown as soon as they went inside.

Frankie Socks noticed.

A few nights a week he would hang out for hours at an all-night diner across from the Mansion like he was watching the place. Mostly he liked being near the

Zimms. They might need him. He owed them a lot. In fact, he owed Dick his life and his freedom.

Socks lived in the Meatpacking District, one of Manhattan's up and coming neighborhoods where ethnic diversity and lifestyle were part of its culture. It was home to artists, many in the LGBT community, and rich and poor alike. The district ran from West 14th Street over to the Hudson River and Hudson Street extending south to the Gansevoort Street Market Historic District.

The neighborhood was busy from early morning, often five A.M., when the warehouse workers began their shift at the plants now surrounded by the growing residential area. From dinner time, to one or two in the morning, later on weekends, the restaurants and bars brimmed with residents and visitors to the city.

What mattered to Socks was he could walk the city anytime, day or night, find places to eat open all night, and have no one notice you unless you decided you wanted that. He didn't.

Socks blended in with little difficulty. How he afforded a lovely two-bedroom apartment was another mystery that most likely wouldn't be solved.

Tonight, he noticed someone dressed in all black, like a ninja warrior running away from the Mansion once the police went inside. Curious, he took out the small digital camera he always carried in his pocket and followed, making sure to snap a shot or two.

Later he explained to Dick, "Seemed suspicious. Figured I'd see what they were up to. After about five blocks they ducked into an all-night deli."

"Who the hell was it?" Dick asked.

"A young woman. I have a photo of her."

Socks clicked on the small camera and showed it to Dick, then emailed it to him and the police. Little did they know it would become a crucial piece of a puzzle that was to have many odd pieces.

While all this was going on, Blinkie, also a Mansion resident, walked up to Red who was leaning against Vincent's information desk that sat in the middle of the entrance area. He wondered what was going on.

"Now what?"

"No one seems to know anything so far. Your buddy Dick is missing and Dora and Zero marched off somewhere arm-in-arm. They seem to be going hunting."

Once a prominent physician, a blinking disorder ended his successful career and in the process his marriage. Blinkie, who lived alone at the Mansion for the past three years, had practically been knocked down by the figure running away as he was returning from a night out with friends.

He once explained to his poker cronies, as they were known at the Mansion, "Don't want a love life so much when you're this old." He grinned, knowing for him that was a lie.

Blinkie was seventy-one and loved the ladies.

Dick once teased him, "You and Bertie should get together."

Blinkie gave him a raised eyebrow, laid down four queens and won a big pot.

Three people bumped into Blinkie as he walked in the front door. He had been getting ready to use his key so there would be no alarm when they practically knocked him over.

"Hey, where you all going?"

He got a quick wave and they rushed away.

There were twelve floors with two and three bedroom condo units at Skyline Vista. All expensive. The top floor had two penthouse units, one belonging to the Zimmerman's, the other to a mysterious gentleman who spent only a few months a year there.

"He looks familiar," Dora mentioned to Dick after bumping into him on the elevator one night.

"Mind your own business, darling." Dick hugged her and went off somewhere or another. He had recognized him also but assumed he wanted his privacy.

On the main floor of Skyline Vista were offices plus the dining area and an exercise center. The second floor had a large room with sliding panels used for a variety of card games, including regular poker games, parties and entertainment. If there were several events or activities going on at one time the panels could separate them.

The third floor had a small store for necessities, a beauty salon, TV area and a library for reading and borrowing books, or just hiding out if one desired.

Dora and Zero made their way down the hall of the fifth floor after finding all was quiet on the fourth floor. "Why is it so much colder on this floor?" Dora asked, rubbing her hands together.

Zero shrugged his shoulders, walked toward the end of the fifth floor hall and pointed to an open door. They knew everyone's doors were locked tight at night.

Except for Bertie Gladstone.

Sometimes she would forget to lock her door. There was also a sign on the door and her doormat that read *Visitors Welcome. Bertie.*

Walking down the corridor, nearing the door, Dora stopped and leaned against the wall, aware she felt uncomfortable. She called to Zero anxiously, "Hold on, I'm not sure we should be up here doing this. Something doesn't feel right."

He knew Dora well enough; she was never an alarmist. He went and stood next to her, waiting for her to make a decision about what she wanted to do.

"I remember when we first moved here, we were strongly advised to keep our doors locked at all times, it being New York City. Of course they did remind us they consider the building very safe, with security and fire alarms, and a manager on duty at all times, day and night."

"I bet Dick had a few sarcastic comments."

"Oh yeah, he hugged me and told me not to worry, that he would protect me. We both laughed when I asked him what if I needed protection from you."

"Come on, Lady D, we're all three of us true New Yorkers. This place is practically in the center of the city. Taxi's almost always out front. Easily a dozen good restaurants as well as bars, and café's are located nearby. It's a short ride to the Village or SOHO for jazz and comedy clubs and specialty restaurants and not much farther to Little Italy or Chinatown going south, or Lincoln Center, the Metropolitan Museum of Art and so much more going uptown. We're in good hands here!"

"You're right. Come on, let's peek in." Dora neared the open door.

Together they marched toward the mystery that would consume them for some time.

"Zero, there's no lights on. It's quiet."

"Move out of the way, Lady D. Let me get ahead of you. We don't know what's happening in there."

The nameplate to the right of the door above the bell buzzer read *Tess and Blanche Martin*.

Dora of course ignored his advice and walked ahead into the dark condo. She bumped into a chair, then felt around and found a small lamp to turn on.

Zero yelled out several times, "Anyone here?"

They looked around the spacious, neat living room and kitchen all decorated in bright shades of yellow. "Wow, kinda bright in this place," Zero said. "All this yellow is like being in a dentist's office."

Zero entered the bigger of the two bedrooms with an adjoining bathroom, the layout being similar to his two-bedroom condo. He continued calling the occupants' names.

The heat had been turned off and the windows stood wide open. It was November and way too cold outside for that. The Zimms would have preferred to be in Vegas this time of year but had agreed to spend Thanksgiving in the east.

With good reason.

Dora and Zero stopped suddenly at the door of the second and smaller bedroom. They stared at the body of a fully clothed man lying in bed. He could have been sleeping except for the very odd looking knife plunged into his chest.

Zero pulled out his cell phone. He kept it near him, always ready to take bets. He dialed the night manager's desk.

"Tell the police to get up to the fifth floor," he told Vincent. "Have them call their headquarters. Someone's been murdered in number 560."

He made several unanswered calls to Dick, each time leaving him the same message.

"Someone's been stabbed. Where are you?"

Dora poked him. "I know he can't be asleep. He just went upstairs."

"Dick, where are you?" Zero said again after the tone.

Grabbing the phone, Dora added, "Dick, darling, where the hell are you?"

Zero added, "Dick, Dora and I found some guy in 560 who is most definitely dead in bed."

It had been exactly 12:05 A.M. when the front door alarm had gone off, blasting through the Mansion. Most seniors in Skyline Vista had been asleep for hours after having an early bird dinner and watching home shopping or some reality show on TV. Not our senior sleuths. Not Zero. Not their cronies. They could gamble or drink or party until dawn and frequently did.

Not this night. There would be none of that.

There was a dead body in 560.

The two young policemen rushed upstairs with Vincent after they called for backup.

Dora and Zero still could not find Dick Zimmerman.

Where were the Martin sisters?

The murdered man was not a resident of Skyline Vista.

"Zero, I know yellow is meant to be cheery, but it's strange in here," Dora said. "They have no family photos, or any books." Eying the heavy lined drapes covering the windows, she added, "It's like they're blocking out the world."

"I know. Like they're hiding something or from someone."

Zero quickly looked back into the other bedroom before the police got there. Rummaging around, he pulled open several dresser drawers.

"I found a few photos."

Dora leaned in to take a look.

"Grab them," she encouraged.

At that moment, he heard the elevator doors open and voices coming toward them. He quickly shut the drawer leaving the photos inside. Zero went to stand near Dora by the bed with the dead man.

Pointing at the large canvas overnight bag by the side of the bed, she asked, "Wonder how long he was planning on being here?"

"Lady D, the police will have to find out from the sisters, who are conveniently missing."

"As is my husband," Dora said, contemplating the body. "That's a truly strange looking knife in his chest."

They would later discover that wasn't the only strange object. The photos resting snug in their drawer would be some of the strangest yet.

Chapter 2

Residents of 560

Holiday lights flickered on and off in store and restaurant windows as Dick Zimmerman walked quickly to Mickey's Bar and Grill with Tess and Blanche Martin.

He was doing his best to calm them down after finding them hysterical at the elevator.

They had walked right into him as he was about to go up to his penthouse condo, intending to remove himself from the chaos of people either annoyed or frightened by the alarm.

They surprised him. A lot, he realized the more he thought about it later.

"What was a gentleman to do?" He wisecracked to Dora, Zero and Detective Donnelly later.

Two doors over from Skyline Vista, Mickey's was a popular hangout for residents who wanted a break from the Mansion. After midnight, the windows had a slight frost on them, making the warmth inside inviting to New Yorkers and visitors alike, most in a holiday mood. Holiday music played in the background and there was an alcohol-induced cheer at the bar. Long past dinnertime, Mickey's bar brought in those who loved the nightlife. Also those people who preferred not to go home. For some the bar *was* home.

The owner, Mickey Donnelly's cousin, Shawn Donnelly, was a damn good New York City detective. Detective Donnelly and Dick had enjoyed the bar, poker nights and a friendship for over twenty years.

Dick directed the hysterical ladies through the old-fashioned style New York pub and restaurant. The bar stretched on the left from the front to the back with red leather stools. Additional seating was on the right with tables and darker red leather seats. Two large round reservation-only tables sat in the back and accommodated up to twelve people.

The tables were rarely empty, including tonight.

The ladies had been hysterical since getting off the elevator. Dick had taken each of them by the arm and rushed them to Mickey's as they babbled on and on about what had happened. At the time it seemed the only reasonable thing to do.

"The women were in distress, what would you have me do?" Dick had shrugged off anything sinister on his part when going over the whole scene later with Donnelly.

Dick directed the two to an empty table recently vacated by a jolly group. He waved away the waitress wanting to wipe it down first. Blanche did most of the babbling.

"There's a dead man in one of our bedrooms. He has a knife in his chest. Who would do that? Oh this is terrible, terrible, terrible. He was such a nice man. So nice, so nice. What are we to do?"

She hardly took a breath between sentences. Tess gave Blanche a dirty look.

"Jealous bitch," Blanche replied.

At the elevator, Dick had wondered about their attire. They weren't in pajamas unlike most of the other residents. Although coatless, each was dressed as if coming downstairs for dinner.

"He's dead. Someone has killed him. They'll think we did it." Blanche continued her drama.

"Ladies, who was killed?"

"Alphonse."

"Who is Alphonse?"

"Her Tango instructor," Tess sniped, pointing at Blanche.

Blanche seemed to shrink even further into the bench seat, tears running down her rouged cheeks.

"Jealous bitch," she repeated.

Dick sat silent, wondering. "How did they have time to fix their faces with makeup?"

"Did you invite him to visit?" Dick asked.

"No," Tess shouted.

"Yes," Blanche whispered at the same time.

"Blanche, why didn't you tell me? How dare you invite someone to my home?"

"Your home now? I thought it was our home. I've paid half the expenses since I moved in so don't give me that B.S. You would have told me no. I knew you would be angry when I told him yes."

"Of course I would have. The man is, was, no good."

Dick downed his second scotch and soda in ten minutes. Although the ladies said they didn't want anything he ordered them both a whiskey, insisted they drink it and only then agreed he would listen to them.

"Blanche, why *did* you invite him?" Dick asked.

"Never mind asking her why," Tess replied, continuing to glare at her sister. "He wanted to borrow money from us. I told him no, but she had such a crush on him, I knew she would agree to help him."

"Blanche, how much money did he want to borrow?"

"Twenty-five thousand dollars," she said softly, almost too softly to hear in the lively bar.

Tess shouted again, "He was a con man. I told you that for weeks."

"I don't care. I liked him and he liked me."

"Are you crazy? He wanted money from us. Probably was planning to rob us too."

"Tess, enough. Blanche, how did you know him?" asked Dick.

"I took Tango lessons from him for the past six months at the Village Community Center. I always wanted to learn to Tango and since I have free time, I thought I would give it a try."

Dick continued to ignore his phone buzzing in his pocket every few minutes. At the same time he realized Blanche and Tess had kicked each other under the table a couple of times.

"Crazy, odd behavior," he later described what went on at Mickey's to Dora, Zero and, of course, Detective Donnelly.

As they went back and forth about Alphonse, Dick watched them. They looked alike, yet different. Each had short dark hair, probably colored for years now, slender and pleasant enough looking. Blanche, definitely more attractive than Tess. Easy prey for a con man if that's what Alphonse was.

"The tango lessons made me happy," Blanche said, sitting up a bit straighter. "I've been lonely since my husband died. Tess, I know you were jealous!"

"Blanche, you're acting crazy."

"Am not."

Dick asked the waitress for another drink, got out his phone and saw all the missed calls and messages. He dialed Zero.

Zero began talking immediately and Dick listened intently.

"I'm at Mickey's with the Martin sisters," Dick finally broke in. "Need you here now. Bring Dora."

He snapped his phone shut. Tess and Blanche continued going back and forth about Alphonse Romero, lover and con man, depending on which sister was speaking. Dick glanced up gratefully as the waitress set down his drink.

Dick learned Blanche had moved in with her younger sister Tess less than three years ago after her second husband of twelve years had died suddenly. They had no children.

She did have children from her first marriage, three in fact, now all grown.

Tess had never married. Claiming "Men are a nuisance."

Dick sat back and sipped his third drink. He watched the door, waiting. Zero soon came bursting in with Dora, furious at his disappearance when there had been a murder at Skyline Vista. They hadn't realized Dick had already been drawn into it.

Dora and Zero had apparently taken time to get out of their nightwear. Dick realized he was still wearing his pajamas but at least he had been able to grab the coat Vincent had hanging on a rack near the door. Not really thinking about his attire, off he went into the streets of Manhattan with two ladies in a state of panic clinging to him.

Dora and Zero knew he was a softy when it came to a woman in need. He could be taken in by tears, sobs, pleas and promises. On the other hand, he could be equally tough and tenacious when seeking the truth.

"You're a clever one." Dora spoke first after Zero and she made their way to his table.

"Running off with not one but two ladies in distress while Zero and I find a dead body, which I assume belongs to them."

Dora's words started Blanche sobbing again and Tess threw her arms up in the air.

"Zero, what's happening back at the Mansion?" Dick asked, ignoring the two ladies' histrionics.

"Dick, my dear," Dora answered while Zero called the waiter over to get a drink himself. Both slipped into the booth. "There is a dead man with a very odd looking knife in his chest, lying on a bed in their home. The police who responded to the alarm called for backup and your Detective buddy, Shawn Donnelly, arrived at the Mansion along with the medical examiner."

Zero leaned in toward Dick. "Wanna take odds which one of these two ladies knocked off the guy, dead in their bed?"

Dora kicked Dick under the table. "Darling, we do need to take these ladies back to the Mansion. The police are looking for them and for you."

"For me? What did I do?"

"My dear, you disappeared right after a man was found murdered."

Dora pointed to Zero, then called the waitress back. "Ma'am, we must leave. Please give the check to this charming and generous patron of ours."

Off the four of them went, leaving Zero laughing and paying the bill.

"Tess, take Dora's arm. Blanche and I will go armin-arm together into the lion's den," Dick said.

He shrugged his shoulders, raised his eyebrows and mouthed to Dora, "Help."

She grinned, knowing he was already in deep; only into what neither of them really had any idea, except it included a dead man.

It would become deeper.

After all few things are as they seem on the surface. Underneath is often a layer of secrets, half-truths and deceptions meant to be misleading. Many meant to cover up misdeeds and hidden histories. This time would be no different.

The Zimms and their pals would find themselves once again involved in more than murder.

Reaching into the pocket of Vincent's coat looking for a tissue to hand the still crying Blanche, Dick found a piece of crumpled paper. Pulling it out, he read a very disturbing message:

Be ready. I'll be there a little before midnight tonight.

Chapter 3

Pocket Full of What?

"Come on, Zero, give me better odds than three to one. I'm telling you one of those not so sweet Martin sisters did in that Tango dancer."

Zero was taking bets over the phone about the murder at Skyline Vista. Who was the murderer? Who was not? How long would it take the Zimms to solve it?

The Mansion cronies, big stakes gamblers, placed money on who committed the murder of Alphonse Romero.

This all within an hour after the body had been found.

"Zero, get back here, police want to talk to you."

Dick phoned him as Vincent was insisting he give him his coat back, practically trying to pull it off him.

Dick pushed him away as if he was swatting a fly.

"Damn it, I want my coat."

"First I have a question for you."

"The day manager is on the way, ask her."

"Nope, I don't think so. She can't help me with this one."

He paused for effect. Vincent felt a knot in his stomach and turned white. Dick put his arm around his shoulder as if he was comforting him.

"Only you can tell me about the note."

Dora watched them from across the room. Vincent had stopped pawing at Dick trying to remove his coat. Dick said something; Vincent paled.

"It's not what you think," Vincent whispered to Dick.

"Vincent, I don't know what to think. Why don't you tell me what I should think?"

Dora slid up next to them, acting all innocent and uninterested. A smart lady, she knew from Dick's demeanor something was going on. Having his arm around the night manager was definitely not something he would normally do.

Dick had never been fond of Vincent. "I find him a bit too cheery and accommodating," he told her. "Seems insincere to me."

At that inconvenient moment Detective Donnelly came downstairs from the murder scene. He looked none too pleased.

"Who's in charge here?"

"Me," Vincent managed to mumble.

Dick still held him. "Hi there, Shawn. Vincent was telling me he wasn't feeling so well. Murder seems to make him sick."

"Vincent, I don't care, get upstairs. Dora, you and Zero too since you found the body. However that happened."

"Mind if I tag along with my wife? You know how fragile she can be in these situations."

Detective Donnelly laughed. "She's a tough lady. Good thing for you."

Dora punched her husband in the arm, lovingly, although none too gently. "Darling, do join us." Whispering, she said, "What were you up to with Vincent?"

Smiling innocently at Detective Donnelly, he whispered back, "Later, dear."

The fifth floor and the Martin sisters' condo had warmed up.

"Someone turned off the heat, figured we better get it back on before we all froze," Dr. Blythe Morrison, the city medical examiner said. "Keeping the room cold was probably meant to confuse the time of death. I'm pretty sure it was at least a few hours ago. Rigor mortis is at the early stages."

Blythe had worked with Dick and Dora many times. She was a no nonsense top city medical examiner who sometimes testified for, and sometimes against, cases Dick brought to trial. Out of court, she and Dora were friends. Whenever they got together for lunch or dinner, they agreed, Dick was not invited.

Blythe and Dora had met over twenty-five years earlier at an event for NYC Professional Women. As chance would have it, they sat next to each other and the conversation had continued with drinks after the event. They learned they had many interests in common. They talked as if they had known each other all their lives and ever since had had many shared lunches and dinners together.

Blythe was almost sixty and had long black hair without a hint of grey, pulled back tight. She had the looks and mannerisms of someone raised with privilege, which was not the case. She had scraped and scrambled her way into medical school and beyond. Having an unusually high IQ of 160 helped. A lot.

Raised in the world of Harlem tenements, her single mother constantly impressed upon Blythe and her younger brother the importance of education. They didn't disappoint her. Blythe's brother and she had both become physicians. He, a successful psychiatrist, loved to tease Blythe about her interest in the dead after she chose to become a coroner. She thumbed her nose at him as she moved up the ranks to become the chief New York City medical examiner.

Although her family moved from Harlem, they never moved from Manhattan.

As if she didn't have enough barriers to overcome, it wasn't easy for a woman of color to succeed where prejudice had existed for so many years.

She also targeted herself by preferring women personally and professionally.

A policeman stood at the door of 560. Crime scene tape had been draped across the door and the sisters, much to their outspoken dismay, would have to find someplace else to sleep.

Nodding to the policeman at the door, Detective Donnelly demanded answers.

"Where were you two ladies when this happened?"

"We were in the other bedroom, arguing at first, then sleeping."

"Arguing about what?"

"Alphonse. The dead man and money."

"I told him I would loan him some money," Blanche explained with what was becoming an annoying whimper.

"And I told her not to. I said he was a con man," Tess replied.

"What made you think that?" Donnelly asked.

"I hired someone to check on his background."

"And?"

"And what? I told you. He was a con man. Had a police record for bilking older women in California out of their savings and their jewelry according to the report I was given. The women refused to press charges. They were too embarrassed."

"Tess, did you tell all this to Blanche?" Everyone turned and looked at Dora as she tossed the question at her.

"Yes. She told me I was a lying bitch. She's decided I'm either a lying bitch or a jealous bitch. I only wanted to protect her."

"Did you leave him alone while you were in the bedroom?" The detective sounded exasperated. Something was bothering him about these two. Their story had too many holes as far as he was concerned.

"You never heard anybody else come into your home after he did?" he asked.

Blanche and Tess glanced at each other, both shaking their heads.

Dick and Dora caught that exchange.

So did Detective Donnelly.

"Hard to believe you wouldn't have heard screaming or a noise."

Dick walked over to Blanche, sat her down on their light green plush sofa with yellow pillows that matched all their walls.

"What really happened?"

Blanche attempted to appear sheepish, after all her babbling drama. She admitted, "Okay, I gave Alphonse a key so he could stay at our place. He said he needed to be out of his apartment for a few days since they were fumigating it."

Tess yelled at Blanche, "Probably fumigating it from him."

"Tess, sit down, I want to hear the rest of this," ordered the detective. "And both of you stop yelling and whimpering."

Dora went and sat down next to the sniveling Blanche while Dick got up to be by Tess, first whispering to Zero, "Don't let Vincent leave this room."

"I let Alphonse in to our place around seven P.M.," Blanche explained. "Tess was in her room reading. She gave me a dirty look then yelled at me. I yelled back until finally we changed into our nightclothes and turned on the television. We always fall asleep watching television."

"You mean you didn't talk to him when he came in?" asked Dick. "I'm finding all this hard to believe, ladies."

"Of course I did. Don't be ridiculous." Blanche managed a weak glare in Tess's direction. "I said hello, showed him which room he could sleep in, gave him clean towels and said goodnight. He thanked me and gave me a hug."

"Why so defiant about that?"

"Because, it shows Tess he really liked me. Because I'm not stupid. I know you all think I was letting him take advantage of me. So what!"

"What woke you up?"

Dora acted as if she was very perplexed. She was rarely perplexed.

"Tess pushed me awake, asking me why it was so cold. Then yelled maybe my boyfriend had turned off the heat."

"Did you go out together to check on what was happening?"

"No. I went out alone at first," Blanche replied quietly.

"How did you find this dead guy in your bed?"

Donnelly was clearly beyond exasperated. More like royally pissed off. He trusted his instincts and these two were putting on an act of exaggerated drama and rehearsed lies.

Giving Donnelly a dirty look, Blanche continued her story. "I saw my bedroom door open and thought maybe Alphonse was awake. I looked in. I was going to ask him if he was okay or needed anything. That's when I saw him in bed with the knife in his chest. I screamed. Tess came running in and agreed with me he was dead."

"Did either of you touch him at that time?""No."

"Tess grabbed me and took me to her bedroom to change clothes so we could go downstairs and ask for help. There. I told you all I know."

Blanche crossed her arms and turned her head away from the group pouting. Dick guided Tess back to Blanche, shaking his head clearly bewildered. "You mean you two changed clothes and put on makeup after seeing the body and before coming downstairs?"

Tess sat down next to Blanche, both calm now, and reached for her sister's hands. "We couldn't very well come downstairs in our nightclothes. That's not something a lady does."

"Goofy," Dick turned and whispered to Dora.

"Dick, shh."

"Don't shush me, darling."

"You two. Be quiet. I'm not through with any of you," Donnelly snapped, clearly frustrated with the whole scene.

Sitting on the bright green sofa, Dora felt the room had an almost eerie feeling as she looked around and again noticed there was nothing personal in the space. It could have belonged to anyone. Anonymous.

The Martin sisters sat silent for the moment.

Zero held tight to a squirming Vincent.

Dick and Dora Zimmerman grinned at each other. They couldn't help themselves. Even murders had the possibility of humoring them. These two sisters were acting absurd and most of what they were saying made little sense.

"Again, did either of you touch or move the body?" Dick asked.

"Goodness, no. We were too scared."

They were sounding so sickeningly sweet.

"By the way, ladies, why didn't you call the police as soon as you saw the body?" Dora asked.

"Oh dear, I guess we were very confused and frightened. We were on our way downstairs to ask Vincent for help when Dick, about to get on the elevator, saw us in distress and took us to Mickey's to calm us down."

"Dick?" Donnelly's tone dropped to a low gruffness.

"Chief, check with your cousin Mickey," Dick replied. "As I've told you, I saw these two ladies as they were getting off the elevator. I brought them to his bar, got us drinks and waited, figuring Zero and Dora would find us soon enough. I didn't know about the body, so don't start with the hampering an investigation jazz. Thank goodness I grabbed Vincent's coat to put on over my pajamas."

Zero tightened his hold on Vincent's arm. He wasn't going anywhere just yet.

Socks had called Dick at least seven times since the police arrived. His message was "Hurry, need to talk to you. Meet me out front of the Mansion."

When Dick could finally get away, he went downstairs to find Socks freaking out.

"I recognized her," he said out of breath although he was clearly just standing there. He latched on to Dick's arm. "It's been many years, but I know it's her."

"Who?" Dick looked at him like he was crazy and tried pulling his arm away.

"Her, the one you walked out of the Mansion with after the alarm went off."

"Socks, which her? I was with two women."

"The slightly taller one."

"You mean Blanche Martin?"

"Yes, damn it."

"Okay, how do you know her? Why are you acting so nuts about this?"

"Her husband. We knew her husband. You and I, we both did."

"Stop keeping me in suspense. Who the hell was her husband?"

Just then Dora came out, calling for him. "Darling, the police insist on speaking with you again. Immediately."

When Dick turned back, Socks was no longer there.

Chapter 4

What's In a Name?

Italian, born in the Bronx, Anthony Ricco knew he was gay from the time he was twelve years old. He just knew. But he kept it to himself. This was not something you ever mentioned in his family. No way.

Leaving home at eighteen, he moved to the San Francisco Bay area, giving himself distance from his family and history. By the time he was twenty, he had his own Latin Lover from Buenos Aries who taught him how to dance the romance of his homeland, the tango. He became Alphonse Romero.

Alphonse fell in love with the movements and mystery of the dance. He found freedom in being able to express so much just through one's body.

He began teaching the tango at dance studios and community centers along with doing performances at events. He also discovered older women adored him. Many took a series of dance lessons, bought him expensive gifts and treated him to fancy dinners. A few invited him to their homes for dinner and to practice the dance. Somewhere in his character was someone who fancied he was owed more than he had and he began stealing their jewelry.

His lover died of AIDS when Alphonse was not quite twenty-seven. For the next two years, he danced and dreamed. He also schemed all he could.

By thirty, he wanted to go home, meaning New York City. He convinced his new boyfriend of one year that a change would be good for them. They drove across country, rented a small, fifth floor one-bedroom apartment in the Meatpacking District with a view of the Hudson and went about finding work and making new friends.

Alphonse was hungry for more. He had something to prove. Being treated with disapproval and disdain left a hole in him. His moral and ethical choices suffered. Like so many others, he was plagued with a determination, and an almost screaming voice which stated "I'll show them."

When he tried to reach out, his parents hung up on him and refused to see him. It had been twelve years and still they could not bring themselves to accept their son. Alphonse embraced the worst version of himself and allowed other's opinions to dictate his behavior. There would be no way he could win.

"Blanche, you're wonderful. Very graceful," Alphonse would praise her.

She was thrilled with each step and every word of encouragement he gave her. She soaked it up.

As Blanche's tango lessons went from once a week to three times a week, his compliments increased. She acted more comfortable around him. Acting being the key to the interaction by both of them.

Alphonse grew more daring.

He lied about being raised in near poverty.

"My family had very little," he would tell her. "One of four children, we all slept in the same room until I finally moved out. I send them some money each month when I can. We love each other very much."

Blanche figured it was a lie. She didn't care. There was no way he could know how clever and shrewd a woman she was. She let him play his little game enjoying the attention and the magic of the tango.

She began by giving him small gifts, but soon they became more and more expensive.

"Something to thank you for being so kind to me," she would tell Alphonse after class. After a few months they would sometimes go to a nearby café when class was over. They both became more and more comfortable with the game between them.

Alphonse showed his boyfriend her latest gift, an expensive Louis Vuitton White Tambour Lovely Cup diamond watch.

"How did she get to have so much money?" he wondered.

At first, he had pretended he couldn't accept it. She continued to insist. "It's the least I can do to repay you."

Alphonse feigned modesty reaching for the beautiful and expensive timepiece. Blanche feigned understanding his modesty.

Lies, upon lies.

Liars, good ones, think they convince others their lie is a truth. But it is only a matter of time before the relationship between them explodes. Usually there is only one winner, and even that is temporary at best.

Alphonse and Blanche, both liars, held secrets that would end without a winner, only losers. Unfortunately other people get caught in the middle. Good people get hurt. Bad people can extract their own revenge and often do.

Tess Martin noticed the watch when she came to meet Blanche and Alphonse for lunch after class one day.

"Nice watch," she practically sneered.

She knew Blanche had given it to him. She'd seen the receipt on her sister's dresser.

Alphonse glared at her, turned away and gave Blanche a hug. "I must go, my dearest," he said.

Even though she wore little jewelry when taking her dance classes, it was hard not to notice the beautiful black diamond pierced earrings she always wore.

"Those are beautiful, Blanche," he had said one day, asking her where she had gotten them. "From a secret admirer?" He pretended to be joking.

"Sort of secret," Blanche responded, coyly turning away.

She knew he would never guess her secret. Like many men, he assumed some man gave them to her but Blanche had resources of her own. She had earned her wealth.

Her first marriage had ended in violence during her thirties. That story was the heart of her secret.

Her husband had never been violent toward her. His nickname was Cutter and police records about mob and mob warfare proved that name fit what he did and did often. His wife before Blanche was part of his story and secret.

So was the death of her second husband, who seemed to suddenly have a stroke and drop dead.

It didn't matter to Alphonse what her secret was.

I want some of her money. I bet she owns plenty of expensive jewelry, he thought often.

He hatched a plan to stay overnight in her home and take what he could. He lathered on the compliments while twirling her around the dance floor and holding her close. Then he mentioned he was hoping to open his own dance studio.

"It would take about fifty thousand dollars, Blanche," he told her. "I have half of it. I know it's a lot but I thought you might be interested in being a part of it."

She wasn't stupid. She knew there was plenty of hustle in Alphonse Romero. The twenty-five thousand he wanted was not a lot to her. Blanche didn't care if it cost some money to have him and the tango in her life. She knew she could end it anytime she wanted.

It was not fine with Tess.

She and Blanche would argue and stop talking to each other for a short time. This went on for a couple months until Alphonse asked Blanche if he could stay with her because he needed to be out of his place for a couple nights. He figured he could steal her jewelry and like the other older women she wouldn't say anything. He had no idea who he was really dealing with.

Several weeks earlier, Tess had decided to do a background check on Alphonse and although the report showed him to indeed be a con man she only gave Blanche a simple warning.

"Blanche, he's only after your money. You're acting like a silly schoolgirl smitten by his charm."

Before slamming the door as she walked out of their apartment, Blanched turned to her. "Shut up, I know what I'm doing."

Each of them had their own agenda. In the end it was a disaster for all of them.

Alphonse's boyfriend knew there was nothing he could do to stop him. He had met a couple guys at a bar in the Meatpacking District who gave him the names of a fence who would be only too happy to buy stolen jewelry from him.

It was too small a world for such things and the strange looking knife in his chest cut short his fantasies and dreams.

Chapter 5

Zero

The unspoiled child of self-absorbed parents, the oldest of five siblings, a brother and three sisters, Zero was the only one who'd achieved success of any kind.

Over the years, his siblings asked him for money and legal help. In return for his generosity, he was all too often rewarded with snide remarks and varying degrees of betrayal. The final one was a devastating blow causing him to lose a business he loved.

He walked away from all of them.

Having enough money to start a new business, Zero opened a pool hall in a bustling Brooklyn neighborhood. He had a back room where on many evenings friendly poker games took place. Those games often included well-known members of the city who preferred no one knew they ever went there. Zero knew how to be discreet.

It was his off-site sideline that made him richer. He was bookie to the city's wealthier citizens and most of them thought nothing of losing thousands at a time. Fortunately for Zero, he knew what he was doing. Most of them didn't lose very often.

He could be a wise guy and was often a bit of a dandy, although to look at his fashion sense at the Mansion it was hard to believe.

Once in Vegas, on a dare from Dick, he wore a leopard print bikini bathing suit to the pool and paraded around like a beauty queen. Secretly, he kind of liked the attention.

Zero, the bookie, soon became the darling of a few senior women living at the Mansion. Someone had actually taken some risqué photos and sent them to a local newspaper.

Dick and Dora couldn't stop laughing.

Zero was married briefly, twice.

Grinning he had told them, "They didn't take."

Years earlier during a night out to dinner, a couple bottles of wine later, he told Dora and Dick about growing up watching his parents struggle to raise their children.

"Somehow they managed, as people do. They survived year in and year out, until one day my father was killed in a delivery van accident. Someone else was driving. The driver survived. I was with them, had to spend several months recovering in a hospital, not being told about my father's passing until I was ready to go home. I was never the same after that accident. I've had to take nerve pills the rest of my life because of the physical damage."

"I know, Zero, I remember you told me you couldn't afford college. It broke my heart. At least we stayed friends."

"We did. Back then I thought my place in life was to be sure my family was taken care of and that they could depend on me. It took me far too many years to realize they could have, and should have, helped. It was too much for the shoulders of one young man."

Zero had told Dora why he was quitting school as graduation day neared. She went on to college and then law school and ultimately become a highly respected judge. They remained friends for life, through all his marriages and divorces, Dora and Dick meeting, getting married and having children and all of them growing older as time does to everyone.

There was hopefully some wisdom that came to them from life lessons.

In his late thirties, Zero became a successful businessman, owning a bar and restaurant near Manhattan's city hall and police headquarters. He dressed in expensive suits with ties and hankies to match.

"Hey, Zero, love your fashion statement today, green suit and all." Dora and Dick would stop in regularly, have dinner and compliment or tease him depending on their mood and of course what he was wearing.

"You two don't know the meaning of style. I've got an image to keep. People expect me to be hip."

Hip he was.

Still, he never did forgive those in his family who had betrayed him, causing him the loss of the business he loved as well as a great deal of money.

Years later they called him for money to hire an attorney for some reason or other, all apologetic. He hung up on them.

"There are some actions not worthy of forgiving," he once said to Dora.

This was one of them as far as Zero was concerned. Right or wrong it was how he felt.

For Zero, when Dick and Dora were in New York, so was he. When they were in Vegas, so was he. The Zimms had been there for him when his family backstabbed him, helping him both legally and with their friendship.

When anyone asked the Zimms for help solving a crime, Zero willingly joined them.

He would joke, "Let me get my Sherlock hat and I am ready to sleuth with you."

Not Frankie Socks, who almost always stayed in Manhattan. He had missed too many years of living where he loved. Although there was that one time he went to Vegas when they needed his help.

To save his sanity during his time in the Witness Protection Program he began taking pictures. One day he opened a small photography studio taking photos of strangers.

Until Dick helped set him free. Dick had discussed them with Dora.

"You know Socks and Zero are never going to be close friends even when helping us solve a crime or two?"

"Dick, I see them as being different in many ways, and funnily similar in some too. Maybe it's because we like and trust both of them."

"True. Socks keeps mostly to himself. Zero loves people and action. Zero has a great sense of humor, a flair for the ridiculous."

"And they both seem to have a criminal underbelly to their lives. Not sure what that says about us." Dora was sitting in bed, propped up against several pillows as she and Dick discussed the characters in their lives.

"Dora, Socks is different. He has no sense of humor, perhaps a bit of irony, and we have a relationship based on the legal system at first, and in recent years a friendly connection of loyalty.

Zero, on the other hand, has a great sense of humor.

Zero poked Dick in the arm one night at a card game, "We better stay fit, or before we know it we'll all be using walkers and asking Bertie Gladstone to go for a walk."

Dick, laughing hard reached over and gave him a kiss on the cheek.

Zero, not one to be undone, got up and grabbed Dick and plunked a huge kiss on his lips.

This was immediately followed by Dora unexpectedly walking in and asking, "You two want to be alone?"

The rest of those playing cards that night came the next time wearing a pair of false red lips saying, "Kissy, kissy, guys."

Humor was much of what helped keep them young at heart. And the action. They loved the action, which sometimes included solving a mystery.

Alphonse Romero's murder at the Mansion was definitely a mystery.

A murder filled with strange characters, suspense, an unusual weapon, a mysterious note in Vincent's coat pocket, an alarm going off past midnight, someone running away, two sisters with very strange behavior and Frankie Sock's cryptic message.

Dick had been the one to get Frankie Socks into the Witness Protection Program years ago. He was able to set him free from that "bleak and confining existence," as Socks described it, several years ago.

"Frankie, your enemies who wanted you dead for being the prosecution's key witness against them are dead."

And with that Dick welcomed him and his new looks back home to Manhattan.

"What the hell did he want to tell me? He really was upset and anxious." Dick was telling Dora about his conversation with him earlier.

The one that had been cut short when Socks suddenly walked away.

Chapter 6

Poker at The Mansion

"Our twice weekly poker nights are a hoot," Zero was overheard telling a few other residents.

There were up to six players and Bertie's son, Carson didn't always play. For one thing he still worked, writing a bi-weekly feature column for a popular daily New York City paper.

Sometimes he couldn't afford to play, either broke or owing too much money already. Bertie still slipped him a few hundred bucks now and then.

"He's my little boy," she'd shout, and then walk off toward any single man who might be nearby.

They were characters, each and every one of them. "I should write a story about all of you," Carson told them one night.

"No way," shouted Blinkie.

"Hey, bet my paper would give me a hell of a bonus for writing it."

"Red, what do you think?"

Red, the only woman in the game, was as good as any of them. She had been a professional poker player in Vegas for years, came back east for a big tournament in

Atlantic City, won a bundle to the chagrin of most of the men, and decided to stay on the east coast.

Now she was in her mid-sixties, with the same flaming red hair she'd since her twenties, thanks to her hairdresser. According to Blinkie and Zero she was "Still a darn good looking dame."

They considered it a compliment. She did too.

Blinkie would sometimes be caught glancing over at her.

"What the heck is that about?" Zero asked him one time.

Blinkie ignored him.

The games were a part of the fabric of their lives for many reasons.

One time at a Mansion holiday dinner, several of the residents discussed the pleasures and values of the game after one resident known for being a disgruntled grouch fussed at them.

"Don't know what the hell you all get out of losing your money to each other."

Zero put his arm around him, slapped the grouch not too gently on the back and replied, "I'm in it for the sex with Red. When she loses she has to date me."

Walking away they laughed so hard, Red, who was sitting nearby, smacked Zero on the head. "Thanks. Now all the old geezers here will think I'm hot stuff."

"We love the game and gambling. Plus, we have great conversations about philosophy and politics, even about religion and life itself," Dick professed. It was more than gambling.

"Yeah. And don't forget when you're done playing and come over to Mickey's for the best food in town."

"Wonderful, we can spend our winnings and drown ourselves in drink over our losses. You're all heart, Mickey," Blinkie chimed in.

For some reason Blinkie lost more often than he won. He didn't care. He had plenty of money and loved being part of the game and the group of card playing cronies.

And then there was Red.

"I've been playing poker since I was a medical intern and that was a heck of a long time ago," she said. "Back then we sure didn't have much money but it helped pass some down times. Not that there was much of it."

One evening, Dora, dressed in a stunning, long sleeve, fitted, black velvet dress with a gold brooch at the right shoulder, home from a museum fundraising event, ended their conversation. Putting her arms around Dick she told the group, "Sorry all of you, taking my man home. We need to get to bed early."

Everyone laughed. They knew what that meant!

Red looked up, raised her eyebrows and grinned.

She also had her secrets.

Chapter 7

Blanche and Tess

"What's with those two dames?"

Dora was stretched out on her bed, hands behind her head, Dick next to her with a book, pretending to read. She suggested he turn it right side up.

"You mean Blanche and Tess Martin?"

"Yes, I mean them, wise guy. Who do you think I mean, Abbott and Costello?"

Putting the upside down book on the nightstand, Dick looked at Dora and laughed out loud. "Okay, okay. I know something is definitely not right with them."

"That's an understatement. What's with the cockamamie story about Alphonse, the tango instructor? Did they read a Do-It-Yourself murder manual?" Dora was gathering steam.

"Their story is bizarre. I've called Zero and Carson to meet us for dinner tonight at Mickey's and brainstorm this conundrum. Meantime, I'll check in with Detective Donnelly in the morning. Maybe he can join us too and you can nose around here with that pretty nose of yours."

"What if—"

"Tomorrow."

With that Dick turned off his bedside lamp, followed by Dora doing the same.

The holiday lights from across the street snuck into their room and then the morning daylight. None of it disturbed them. It was past fourA.M. when they turned in. Only the phone ringing mid-morning woke the pair of senior sleuths.

"Hey, get down here for breakfast. The whole place is aflutter over your nighttime romp with the Martin sisters." Zero was laughing, reminding Dick he wanted details.

Grumbling, Dick told him the plans for the evening, got up, turned on the coffeemaker, always readied the night before, took a shower and listened to the news.

They were giving whatever details they had about the murder at Skyline Vista Condos. "An exclusive, fancy, expensive, bizarre murder," the perfectly coiffed newswoman said. "At this time we have no new information from the police." Turning to her co-host she replied, "Resident Bertie Gladstone, eighty-nine years old, was overheard asking one of the newspaper reporters for a date. What kind of crazy place is this?" Both grinned at the camera.

At that Dick turned off the TV and got ready to meet his adoring public.

Dora quickly had her own shower, got dressed and had a quick cup of coffee. She was out the door with a brief good morning kiss.

Dick knew Dora was on the hunt for something about the murder. Wearing expensive black slacks and sweater, Gucci leather boots and a black jacket, she was like a panther ready to attack.

"God, I love that woman," he said, smiling to himself.

Dick had his own hunting to do. He picked up the phone. "Hey, Shawn, can we meet for lunch?"

"I didn't know you cared?"

"Lunch. one P.M. at the University Club."

Both hung up without another word.

Going downstairs, Dick was the center of attention most of the morning.

"How did you find the body?"

"Did one of the sisters kill him?"

"Who was the guy murdered in their bedroom?"

Zero pulled him aside, poking at him for information. "What did those crazy sisters have to say last night?"

"Not here, dear boy. Tonight at Mickey's."

The Martin sisters had spent the night on a couple of the sofas in one of the Mansion lounge areas.

They refused to go to a hotel. They were furious.

"What if we need something from our home? We have to stay here. Yes, we know we're not allowed to go in there for now, but *if* we want something? We do hope you can get it for us," Tess complained to a temporary night manager. Vincent disappeared after the police interrogated him.

Putting on his heavy, dark grey cashmere coat, grey and red plaid cashmere scarf and dark grey leather gloves, Dick escaped to meet Detective Donnelly.

No wonder Bertie Gladstone had a crush on him. He looked positively dashing.

"Shawn, did you get any information from the Martin sisters," Dick asked? Shawn checked the menu, deciding between the daily specials of braised lamb chops with mashed sweet potatoes, or shrimp in a curry sauce with rice. Each brought with it a delicious dessert.

After giving the waiter their orders, Dick persisted, "Shawn, Martin sisters? I know you're stalling. Come on, give."

"Dick, I questioned them again this morning. Their story seems like a big fish tale to me, yet they are sticking to it with very few changes. Sounds rehearsed. They kept claiming they were innocent of any wrong doing and acting very confused about what happened."

"You don't believe them?"

"Hard to."

"We're running some background checks, something damn odd about all this. I assume you and your clever and charming bride are trying to figure out this mess since you got caught up in it."

"Yes, she is," Dick said grinning.

"I'll try to join all of you at Mickey's tonight."

Agreeing to keep each other informed of any new information, they left after a delicious lunch, making it easy to go out into a cold New York winter day.

The holidays in New York City brought decorations at every turn, n the store windows, on street lamps tied with large red ribbons, and the beautiful tree in Rockefeller Center ready to be lit the first week of

December. Across from the tree sat the majestic St. Patrick's Cathedral. High above the center of 57th street and Fifth Avenue was a beautiful, huge crystal snowball.

Farther uptown was a famous toy store, and then Temple Emanuel, a large menorah in front decorated with blue ribbons. There was always more to enjoy and appreciate in Central Park with horse and carriages waiting for tourists or lovers, the magic of Lincoln Center on Broadway as a seeming entrance to the west side heading toward Columbia University and on to the Riverside Church where there was a fabulous New Year's Eve service each year.

Paris wasn't the only city of lights. New Yorkers knew better.

"Carson, we need a tiny, little favor from you."

Dick gave him a rundown on the events of the previous evening as Carson sat back with his arms crossed as if protecting himself for what was to come. He knew the Zimms and Zero were up to something, more than a tiny, little request. He was already thinking about what he would want in return. A grin beginning to appear the more they talked.

Zero ordered a bottle of fine wine and appetizers while Dora sat back and waited.

She had some interesting information for them.

Mickey's Bar and Grill was full as usual at dinnertime. They had reservations and prepared themselves for the steak and fries special, and how they might convince Carson to help them.

"How little is this favor?" he asked. He knew all three of them and he suspected it was a big one.

Dick proved he was right.

"We need a deep background check on the Martin sisters. They're acting all confused and innocent. We're not buying it. Before they bumped into me getting off the elevator I heard one of them say something about 'our story' and then broke into their crying and confused act when they saw me."

"Don't forget Vincent. He was quite suspicious acting last night according to you."

"Right. Check on Vincent, Vincent Blair."

"How deep?" Carson was grinning at them. He had figured out what he wanted in return.

"All the way. Marriages, in-laws, parents, business connections, any legal actions against either of them the past twenty, thirty years at least."

Zero added, "I'm not sure what's with them. One time I saw Blanche intentionally trip some man in the lounge. She said it was an accident. I saw it. Believe me it was no accident. She's one mean lady."

"Zero, didn't you say anything to her?" Dora looked surprised, knowing how outspoken he could be at times.

"Nah. She seemed apologetic and put on that same confused act like Dick said she did last night."

"The man she tripped wasn't so forgiving though," Zero said. "Apparently they'd had run-ins with each other before. He was yelling at them, 'What do you two want from me? Keep this up and I'll report you to the police.'"

Zero explained the women never said another word until he walked away, then they started laughing. "One month later, he moved out. Left for California. Seems he wanted to get far away from them."

Dinner arrived and they ordered another bottle of wine. They fell into a comfortable silence, the food too delicious to spoil with conversation.

During dessert and gourmet coffee, Carson sat back on the red leather seat, stretched out his legs and sighed. "Deep background, huh?"

"Yes," all three replied.

"And I'm willing to do this because…"

Dora smiled and said, "Because you love us, dear sweet man."

"Not that much, sweet lady." He grinned at her, even gave her a wink.

"Here's my bargaining chip for you gambling people," Carson said, leaning back, his hands behind his head. "First I want all my I.O.U's gone from the poker games. Zero, you also cancel any debts I have with you for betting the horses." Carson looked smug, made his demands, then leaned in to start on his dessert and coffee.

"What?" Zero shouted.

Dick put his arm around Zero encouraging him. "Take one for the team, buddy."

"What team? And what the hell are you and Dora giving up?"

"Ah, I was getting to that," Carson said. "I expected you wanted something big from me."

"What would that be?" Dora asked slipping into lawyer mode. Dick knew Carson was smart even if he was a rotten poker player.

"I am suggesting a complimentary dinner here at least once a month for, oh let's say six months."

"What?"

Zero cracked up laughing. "Dick and Lady D, do take one for the team."

Carson would find plenty of information on the Martin sisters and their family ties. Enough to write a murder mystery.

How they kept their story under the radar for so many years was another mystery.

Earlier, Dora had done some of her own sleuthing at the Mansion. She knew the Martin sisters' condo was still off limits, but she wanted a better look at those photos in Tess's top drawer.

Both sisters continued to sit in the Mansion's lounge, moaning and complaining. This time they spoke to Bertie Gladstone and anyone else who would listen.

Not too many were willing anymore and Dora knew she had better act fast.

Dora leaned over and whispered to Bertie, "Keep them busy until I come back and sit down with you again."

She hurried upstairs and snuck into their condo. She wanted those photos Zero said he saw. Ruffling through the drawer, all she found was silk pajamas. The photos were gone. Maybe Zero could remember exactly who was in those pictures.

Sitting with the sisters waiting for Dora, Bertie offered so much sincere sympathy it oozed out of her. "Oh dears, how awful for you to have found that body in your home. Was it someone you knew?"

They sat quietly with weak smiles, not revealing anything.

Soon enough bits of truth would begin to drop into the cracks of their lies.

Dora returned to Bertie. The sisters glanced back and forth at each other, grabbed hands, and pretended to stifle a cry. Bertie and Dora noticed all their fake histrionics.

Not a whole lot was completely clear at this point, but the truth ran deep and dangerous.

Chapter 8

Sleuthing

"Darling, there are rules for sleuthing."

Dick thought he was being charming.

Dora thought he was being annoying.

"Don't be ridiculous."

They were in their living room after meeting with everyone. Dora stretched out on the pale blue sofa covered in expensive fabric. Dick faced her, drink in hand, sitting on one of the two matching chairs in a deep cream color. An assortment of beautiful tables placed for the convenience of setting down drinks sat around the room. When they were home at the same time, cocktails and talk usually preceded dinner. They had so much in common, from politics to religious attitude, to professional and worldly interests, Dick and Dora were never bored with each other.

Their condo was high enough they could see west to the Hudson River and east to the East River and FDR Drive, which usually flowed with traffic. They lived in a world of both beauty and danger, of simple pleasures and complex problems.

Their talks might seem to others as intense debates, each presenting a personal perspective on whatever topic was at hand.

Today it was sleuthing.

"See, my dear, one cannot investigate simply because you don't like someone," Dick said.

"Of course one can," Dora replied sarcastically.

The more they disagreed, the more they enjoyed it.

"I'll tell you what. Why don't we review what we each have found out since the murder in the Martin sisters' condo?"

Dora agreed and began before Dick could start.

"There are a number of suspects which of course include the sisters. They say they had no reason to kill Alphonse, and continue to claim their innocence."

"There was jealousy between them, how's that for motive?" Dick tossed in a quick comment.

"Not good enough. It's deeper, more sinister."

"Such as?"

"Dick, consider how they reacted to the questions Detective Donnelly asked them, so child-like. Meantime, they get dressed and put on makeup while a dead body is in the other bedroom."

"True. I've been wondering if they know Vincent outside of his role as the night manager here." Dick took a few quick glances toward her. He finished his drink, set it on the table and agreed the Martin sisters' behavior was a problem. So was Vincent's.

Dora and Dick trusted each other. They had great respect for each other's intelligence and opinions. This type of back and forth, they knew, gave voice to better insights and hopefully offered clarity toward a problem.

"Okay, let's move on to Vincent and the person who set off the alarm."

"Dick, finding that note in his coat pocket made him very nervous."

"Do we know yet who wrote the note? Was it a he or a she?"

"It's unsigned. Vincent wouldn't tell me who wrote it but Socks took a photo of a young woman running away after the alarm went off."

Dick grinned. He still had the note and he handed it to Dora as he leaned over to kiss her on the cheek. For some reason he wasn't ready to show it to Detective Donnelly.

"What about Socks freaking out at seeing them?"

"Damn strange. I left him a message to meet me. He hasn't called back. Dora, I swear seeing them nearly scared him to death."

Dora sat back and looked at her husband of forty years. He was the love of her life. Over the years they had grieved the loss of their parents, almost lost one of their children to cancer, gratefully in remission for many years, and even survived death threats from a few in prison because of one or the other of them.

Dick's parents had relatives who had not survived the Holocaust. "They waited too long to leave," his father told him, the pain obvious as they would go to synagogue and say a prayer for the dead each year on Yom Kippur.

It had had a lifelong impact on Dick and Dora.

Dick and Dora Zimmerman's life's work had been about finding and defending truth and justice.

Sometimes it was difficult.

The murder of Alphonse Romero had plenty of suspects to consider.

Chapter 9

Questioned

Detective Donnelly questioned the staff and residents of the Mansion. Everyone had an excuse, or an alibi, at the time of Alphonse Romero's murder.

Through his tears and grief, Alphonse's distraught lover gave him a list of places where Alphonse had worked, who their friends were and where his family lived in Brooklyn.

When Detective Donnelly called to tell them their son was dead, they replied, "He's been dead to us for years," and hung up.

No one seemed to know anything about who could have murdered him or even why.

The only one who seemed genuinely sad about it was his boyfriend.

The police had a number of suspects. Donnelly had a lot more questions in addition to who had murdered him.

Whose knife was in his chest?

How did the murderer get into the Martin sisters' condo?

Could Alphonse have let someone in without their knowing about it?

Did one or both of the sisters murder him?

What was going on with Dick and Vincent?

How did it happen Dick was getting on the elevator as they were getting off?

How did the sisters have time to change clothes and put on makeup?

Who set off the alarm earlier before the body was discovered?

What did they want?

Was it a resident or someone coming to do some harm?

The medical examiner said there was no doubt the stabbing had killed him.

But…

But, what?

Dora and Blythe Morrison met for an early breakfast. They had their own observations.

"Dora, I'm confident he knew the person who murdered him," Blythe said. "The stabbing happened when someone was quite close to him. I still have to finish the autopsy. He had no defensive wounds, no bruises or scratches of any kind. I'm sure he was drugged first. There's a needle puncture wound at the side of his neck."

Dora respected Blythe's perspective on a case. She rarely, if ever, missed the little things, the finer points of anyone's death. Including this one.

"Detective Donnelly told Dick he sent the knife to the forensic lab. When you get a chance, let me know if they found any prints or identifying markings on it," Dora requested. "Oh, and what kind of drug was injected."

Blythe got up, reached over, hugged Dora and grabbed the check on her way out.

Dora laughed.

They had been fighting over who paid the check each time they went out together for years.

The office of the chief medical examiner can provide information on forensics, autopsies, and even missing persons. It's important someone identify the body. That means showing their personal identification.

The law states:

Anyone who had died as a result of violence or a crime such as murder must be autopsied by the medical examiner. The autopsy shows cause of death and only after that can the body be released for burial or cremation.

In this case, Dr. Morrison was personally handling the autopsy at the request of Detective Donnelly. As a favor to Dora, she had made it a priority.

"Some forensic results won't be in for several days, even with a rush on them. The drug was definitely a huge dose of cocaine."

"So he actually died before being stabbed?"

"Oh yeah, looks like it was almost a ritual killing."

Blythe Morrison had called Dora and Detective Donnelly to come over to see something she described as "Very odd. You need to see this yourselves."

Pulling the white cloth back from Alphonse's body and pointing to the x-ray, she said, "First, take a look at this."

"Diamonds?"

Donnelly leaned over to look closer at the body, then back up at the x-ray, stunned. Dora was on the phone calling Dick about this latest bit of information.

"Sweetheart, you won't believe this."

"Seems they were stuffed down his throat," Blythe said.

"Can you get them out for me?" Donnelly asked stepping back and taking a deep breath. He knew there was a lot more to what was going on with this murder.

The diamonds would be given to the detective. He would have his precinct help check out where they came from, if they had been stolen, anything at all they could learn about them.

Alphonse's boyfriend was waiting for his body to be released.

"His family refused to talk to me. When you're done I want to cremate him," his boyfriend said. "Then I think I'll pour his ashes on the S.O.B. parents' front lawn."

There simply was no comment to that decision.

Chapter 10

The Note

Dick left a message for Vincent. "Be at the diner nine A.M. tomorrow. If you don't show up the note goes to the police."

Vincent was sitting in a booth, head in his hands, almost trembling when Dick arrived. Snow had continued overnight and the streets were wet and slippery. Taxis flew carelessly over them on to their next destination, their next fare.

"She works for us. I mean me."

"You meant us. Who is she? Who is us?"

"I can't tell you, Dick. They'll kill me. In fact they probably will anyhow."

"Why would whoever they are want to kill you?"

"This is much bigger than it looks."

"Meaning?"

"It's not only about someone being murdered at the Mansion."

"So what does it mean?"

"I told you. I can't tell you, or they'll kill me."

"If you don't tell me, I'm liable to kill you."

"No. You won't. You might get someone to arrest me. Not kill me."

"Okay. Let's start this way. The people you're afraid of, do they live at the Mansion?"

"Some of them do."

"Some of them? What the hell is this? A gang of thieves and murderers?"

"Dick, please, I need to go. I told you too much already."

"Vincent, I'll arrange for Detective Donnelly to protect you."

"No one can protect me."

"What does that mean? It makes no sense."

"It would if you knew what I know."

Vincent stood up. "Do what you want with the note. Doesn't really matter anymore. I can't stay here. I have to go."

"Go where? Tell me what's going on. Let me help you."

"You can't. No one can."

Vincent was out the door and gone.

He had been right, no one could help him.

Chapter 11

Never Too Old

There were all sorts of secrets at the Mansion, including a few romances. There were also enough gossips including the formidable Bertie Gladstone to share the secrets.

It was difficult for Bertie to leave the Mansion very often. Her grandson Carson would sometimes take her over to Mickey's or across the street to the diner for lunch. Dressed up, waiting in the lounge, she would say she had a hot date.

Residents like Bertie who were not mobile enough to wander around the city or go out much found other ways of filling the void in their lives. She was smart and inquisitive. She watched others, pretending she was dozing when in fact she was listening to a conversation. There were secrets yet undiscovered like residents in love.

Bertie laughed when confronted once about being a busy-body.

"I quite enjoy it," she said. "This place is filled with mysteries and sex."

A couple people sitting with her were shocked and walked away. Others laughed. They knew she was right.

Bertie had a mild to major crush on almost every unmarried man and then there was Dick Zimmerman. She told him he was extra special and giggled.

The Zimms adored her.

"She's my role model," Dora said. "When I'm eighty-nine I expect to be as feisty."

"Dora, darling, you are feisty enough for me now." Dick hugged her.

Red and Blinkie met at the Mansion poker game a few years back. He immediately fell for her red hair and obvious intelligence. It surprised the hell out of him. Out of both of them. It had been years since anyone held his heart like that. Red was also surprised at her own enthusiastic response.

Their non-secret romance, going on six months, allowed for some darn funny comments amongst the natives.

"Do you think they're doing it?"

"They're too old."

"You nuts? Little blue pills keep you young."

"Hey, sweetie, I can get me some little blue pills."

"Go away."

"How old do you need to be to get them?"

"You're old enough."

"Stay away from me. I want someone younger than you."

That last comment was from Bertie Gladstone.

Red and Blinkie ignored the gossip and innuendos. Blinkie especially ignored all and any snide comments from Dick and Zero. They had figured it out almost from the beginning.

Blinkie had lived a good life, making plenty of money as a physician. He loved poker, sports, the opera, and Red.

The murder at the Mansion ended a number of secrets. Not only Red and Blinkie's but a few of the other employees and residents including the Martin sisters and the mysterious tenant in the other penthouse condo.

"Dora, of course there are different types of secrets," Dick told her. "People who want to hide a crime, a romance, something personal that happened to them at one time and want to keep it private. What about someone living a lie and not wanting others to know? In court people lied all the time. Even some clients you defended lied."

Dora and Dick were having dinner alone at their favorite restaurant in Chinatown. Ducks hung in the windows, and the streets were packed with holiday shoppers and visitors.

The owner welcomed them with a hug. They had been patrons for years. Sometimes they joined the owner and his family for a huge Chinese New Year feast that took place in February.

The hot and sour soup arrived, warming them. The howling wind outside made it seem colder than it actually was. Most people were bundled up with scarves and gloves and heavy coats. Although New York was usually a city for walking, this night was not.

"Secrets can also be much darker than that," Dick said in between spoonfuls of soup.

"Meaning?"

"People we've dealt with in our professional lives. Criminals. Gamblers. Pedophiles. Thieves. Sociopaths and psychopaths that are compulsive liars."

"Yes. Don't forget murderers."

"Dora, my dear, hard to forget them." Dick leaned over and kissed her.

They had few if any secrets from each other. After forty years of marriage, their only indiscretions had been moments of Dick's excessive gambling or Dora having once spent several months talking to a therapist when their son had been ill. Gambling was in a way Dick's therapy and Dora understood that. She was fine with it.

Dora had been left a great deal of money. She understood all too well how everyone deals with pain or hurt or loss in their own way.

This night Dick did have a sort of secret.

He had been aware of two men following them since they left home. They got in a taxi after he and Dora had, and got out in Chinatown right after they did. Pretending to go up to the front to get some matches from the counter, he saw them hidden in the doorway of a nearby closed tobacco shop across the street.

His biggest concern was Dora would go out and ask them what the hell they wanted and they might respond by shooting them.

Not a good plan.

He went over to the owner of the restaurant, whispered what was happening, and agreed one of the waiters would create a diversion when they left. Dick ordered a Town Car to take them home.

"Much too cold to hope for a taxi," he told Dora. "I've called for a car to take us back to the Mansion."

As Dick and Dora got into the Town Car, a waiter ran outside, screaming there was a fire at the back of the restaurant. Curious people on the street stopped and crowded the area, preventing the two dark figures from following Dick and Dora.

"That was brilliant, darling." Dora sat back and laughed.

"What was brilliant?"

"Creating a clever diversion so those two men wouldn't be able to follow us when we left."

Dick burst out laughing too.

"Yes, dear, only we have to figure out who they are and why they would be following us. I sent an email to Donnelly about our groupies."

Chapter 12

Once Upon a Romance

Old wounds swirled around Red often over the years. Believing and trusting in love had been difficult. Maybe it was age. Maybe it was simply time.

Still she remembered.

Tommy got married.

She had heard the words. They rang in her head. Even now a lifetime later she remembered those words, that moment, the silence at the table, everyone looking at her.

"Tommy got married."

Red was with a group of college classmates at a local hangout where they enjoyed beer, music, dancing and more beer. They were sitting at one long table by the end of the dance floor. How do you forget a moment like that? A moment that took your breath away and changed your view of love and relationships.

Red remembered that night the rest of her life. She was nineteen. Tommy and she had been dating for over a year. Trouble? He was Catholic and she was Jewish. Families on each side were determined to have it end. It was a time when mixed marriages were considered a death knell for some families.

"I love you," he told her.

"I love you too. My parents are going crazy over this Tommy. I don't know how long I can keep fighting them."

It ended for a while after months of fights, tears and promises to her parents she would take a break from seeing him at the end of the school year and see what happened.

The inevitable happened.

Tommy started dating others.

He was a handsome, nice Italian boy that brought plenty of interest from nice Catholic girls.

He had told her, "I'm mad. Our parents aren't right."

"I know."

They started seeing each other again the following school year, then stopped forever before the New Year began.

Tommy and his summer girlfriend got married the following spring. It felt awful to Red.

Sadly a few other young girls she knew had similar experiences.

"Marry your kind," they were told. "It's a sin to not marry someone Jewish. You'll break our hearts."

Guilt.

That was their parents' best weapon.

Red told Blinkie her story one night when they had been sitting at Mickey's. "I later married, divorced, moved to Vegas and learned to be a first rate poker player. It was my revenge against what was expected of me. I revolted from being a traditional Jewish wife. It wasn't for me."

Blinkie had reached over and hugged her. They ordered after dinner drinks and he let her finish telling him what happened, so long ago, yet still to her it was a love lost. Long ago didn't matter.

"I saw Tommy with his wife a couple of times. It was awkward. A nod hello once, none after that."

"Tommy got married."

That late spring night, in the bar, she was silent at the announcement.

It was years later, after a college reunion she had not attended she got a phone call.

"I thought about you a lot all these years," Tommy told her.

"I wondered what you looked like."

"The same, older."

For several months they spoke, maybe once a week. Memories, that's all it was.

Memories of their first dates, their first kiss and more.

Memories reminding her of when she heard he got married. Now with four children he was still living in the very blue-collar eastern city where they had grown up and met.

"I thought of you when I saw the movie *Dirty Dancing*. It reminded me of you, of us."

Red listened. What was there really to say after so many years?

"I saw you once on a date with some other guy. I was actually jealous." He laughed, an embarrassed laugh.

She reminded him of their accidental meeting in the La Guardia airport on her way upstate.

"You're staring at me."

It had taken her a few minutes and she was sure it was Tommy.

"What's your name?"

Surprised, he said, "Tommy. Why?"

"Don't you know who I am?"

Bewildered he stared at her again. She knew she looked damn good.

Much slimmer than college days. Long red hair, down the middle of her back, wearing an orange and cream-colored linen dress that came to her knees.

He finally realized. "Red?"

"Yes. I thought you knew, the way you were looking at me."

"That's because I saw a good looking woman, hard not to stare."

She relished that moment. *A moment of revenge*, she thought, Tommy having a bit of a pouch belly and four children.

"Can I call you sometime?"

"No."

Now, years later, their renewed connection ended same as their love had years before.

One day it was over. The talks stopped. He was still married. She never went out with married men.

Red was sure he never realized what she once told a good friend.

"He was the love of my life."
In her sixties something had suddenly changed.

Chapter 13

Disappeared

"Dick, please find V." Vincent only had minutes to make the phone call before they knocked on his door and he would be gone. Forever. He finished leaving his message and hung up.

The phone went dead soon after Dick picked up the call. He listened to Vincent, then called Donnelly to play the message for him, telling him, "Possible abduction. Possible murder."

It was already too late for Vincent. He was a dead man from the minute he was picked up at his apartment by two men and driven away in a dark four-door sedan. He knew these people, who they were, and what they were capable of doing.

These were the same two men who had followed Dick and Dora to Chinatown.

Vincent had screwed up big time regarding the murder at the Mansion. They would see to it he disappeared. He was hoping to protect her.

They had grown up together, worked together for years along with their brother who was eight years older than Vincent. The family saw to it. In the beginning it was small time stuff. As they got older that changed. As young teenagers they were taught the family business, to explicitly follow the family's instructions.

Those instructions included never letting anyone get near the family, never let anyone know about the family. It's as if they were a secret society, certainly living under the radar, by their own rules, expectations and demands.

To defy them, or ignore them, or create a problem for them would not be tolerated.

Vincent and V had always been careful.

They had never been caught. As teenagers they were told never to mention their brother. They had no idea he was in prison.

How could they know the problems Alphonse would cause them?

"Damn that Alphonse. We need to figure out what to do about him."

They had warned him. He wouldn't listen. V was meeting with Vincent. She had a lovely apartment in the West Village. Located in lower Manhattan bordering Greenwich Village and Chelsea neighborhoods, it was an expensive, mostly residential area, and like most of Manhattan there were many shops and restaurants, small cafés and easy access to the subway system.

She often yelled at Vincent, "You need to invest your money in a nice apartment. Stop taking chances with it."

He felt no need for that and instead invested his money in the volatile stock market. "I like the challenge, V. It's the once place in my life I can do what I want."

Still, he had plenty of money. His will left whatever he had to V.

"Does she ever talk to you about him?" Vincent stood up to get a beer, waiting for V to answer.

"Not lately. Since she moved in with Tess, she's been much more cautious." She asked Vincent to bring her a beer too.

"What do you think that's about?"

"She once told me Tess has a bad temper. Doesn't want her involved in everything happening with the family."

"You gotta be kidding. Ever experience Blanche's temper? Remember when we were young. Hell, she almost threw me out a third floor window when I said no to her for some reason."

V laughed. "I remember." She had a great laugh.

Vincent thought she could have done something wonderful with her life, if she had been born to another kind of family, a family that valued education and creativity, love and kindness.

They loved each other. Protected each other.

Sometimes they would sneak off to a museum or art gallery and look at the beauty for a brief time.

One time they went together to watch a Three Stooges film marathon in Greenwich Village, probably the most they had ever laughed.

Their family, what could they say?

"You know the murder of Alphonse is going to cause us problems."

"V, he brought it on himself. I told him to stay away after he approached me. I told him he was dealing with dangerous people. He laughed. Said I was being selfish, wanting everything for myself."

"You warned him, right?"

"I did."

"So?"

"Was Alphonse only after some money and jewelry?"

"V, he had no idea about anything else."

"Blanche is the one who has really caused the problem, letting this guy too close so she could take those stupid dance lessons."

"Tess warned her but she figured she could handle him." V got up and hugged Vincent; they both knew what was coming.

"After he saw me talking to a couple guys in the Meatpacking District he realized he knew them too. He had fenced some jewelry with one of them that he had stolen when in California."

"Did you tell Blanche?"

"No way, she was raving about how happy she was with her tango lessons and instructor and that she might even open a studio with him. She would have been furious with me for even bringing it up."

"I guess she reached an age of feeling she was in no way vulnerable to her past. Hard to know what else made her act so irresponsibly?"

"V, you need to see if you can get away."

"I was supposed to leave the front door unlocked so V could get in and help me handle something for the family. When the alarm went off, I knew I was in trouble. The alarm, as you know, caused a lot of attention and brought the police. Then your wife and Zero found the body."

Vincent took a deep breath, put his cell phone and wallet on the table, he wouldn't need them, and finished his message to Dick.

"I made a stupid mistake. Without the alarm happening, Alphonse's body would have disappeared. Dick, I killed Alphonse with a knife from a collection of them hidden away. I had no choice. They always kept me in check by threatening to hurt V if I didn't do what they told me to…for the family. Dick, V is my sister."

Dick replayed the message, stunned. It didn't matter who else listened to it. At least it didn't for Vincent.

Hopefully they could still find and help V.

Chapter 14

It Was a War

"It was wartime."

Frankie Socks met Dick at a café in the Village. It was dark out by five P.M. Even with all the holiday lights blinking on and off an eerie almost ominous presence hung in the air as they sat sipping coffee.

Dick let him take his time, to play it out in his own words. He knew what wartime meant to Socks. He had been there to save him. For some reason he liked the guy, maybe he saw a bit of himself reflected back. He hadn't figured out exactly what part that was.

"Maybe I'm just a bleeding heart lawyer," he told an FBI agent. "He'll talk if we promise to get him into the Witness Protection Program. We need his testimony against the mob."

Socks had enough information to get a whole lot of the mob locked up for a long time. They wouldn't hesitate to knock him off and make sure he was never found.

After the trial and his testimony, he was immediately put into an unmarked van, driven to a private airport, handed papers with his new name, a wallet with some cash, a small limit credit card, and the name of a plastic surgeon that had been paid to make his face look different. Once that was done he would have his photo taken to get a driver's license and passport matching his new name and face.

The feds had also opened a small bank account in his new name and arranged for an apartment in a pleasant enough community somewhere in the middle of America.

The agent was less than thrilled. Didn't matter. Dick made it happen. Over the years he would get cards with encrypted messages knowing they were from Socks. A photo inside with a note always saying the same thing: *Wish you were here*.

The cards made Dick laugh. He knew he'd be able to find Socks when it turned out it would be safe for him to come back to New York City.

Socks shook his head, back and forth, left to right, left to right. "Like all wars there were more losers than winners," he said.

"You know what I mean?"

Dick nodded. "Yes, it makes sense."

Socks had been a good-looking man when he was younger. Well built, with the greenest eyes. The ladies wanted him. So did the bad guys but for different reasons. He had been a member of a mob involved in drug trafficking and prostitution.

They all knew each other as young kids growing up in public housing, most with little parental supervision. The few whose parents tried usually lost to gangs controlling their neighborhoods, instilling an intense sense of fear.

When Socks had been arrested he told the police, "I was the driver for the head of one of the mobs, dragged into the life by my older brother. I never wanted or liked it."

It didn't take a lot to convince him to be a witness for the prosecution. His brother had already been killed in the mob wars along with some of his other friends.

He'd had enough and that had been almost twenty years ago.

Dick was watching him, listening to him. He tried to remember what he used to look like.

Socks saw Dick drifting away and banged at the table. "You gotta listen to me."

"Why? What's going on here, Frankie?"

"The trouble with any war is it's devastating. It leaves behind the loss of life, betrayals and painful memories for survivors. History proves wars are a senseless waste of humanity's efforts and energies. The cost in every way is beyond comprehension."

Dick was nodding his head in agreement. *Please, please get to the point you want to make already*, he thought.

Socks was getting there.

"That war I was in, it was not so different. Motivated by greed, power and ambition."

Dick had put away quite a few who survived those wars, only to die in prison. It had been a mob war for who would control drugs and prostitution in all five boroughs of New York. For months, members of one group killed members of another keeping the police busy picking up after them. The retaliation continued until

Frankie Socks was arrested and agreed to testify. Socks was really not a bad guy. At least he never killed anyone.

Socks finally finished his war story and shouted at Dick, "Listen to me. We got a problem."

"What kind of problem?"

"When I saw you walk out with them, I freaked out, couldn't believe it was her."

"Was who? Which her?"

"It's been a long time. I'm good at remembering faces."

"So, whose face did you see last night?"

"The woman who used to be Cutter's wife."

"What are you talking about?"

"Blanche Martin."

"Remember he was head of the downtown mob. They called him Cutter. He killed people by stabbing them. Said he didn't like guns. Go figure that one out."

"Are you sure?"

"Of course, I'm sure!"

Dick quickly pulled out his cell phone, dialed Carson Gladstone, and said, "I need you to find out what you can about a mob figure from twenty years ago called Cutter. Dead now. Check out family ties, living or dead. As soon as possible."

Then he called Detective Donnelly and in five minutes told him what had taken Socks an hour to tell him.

"Socks, go home. Stay away from here. Call me tomorrow morning."

"This was bad," Dick thought.

Really bad.

If Blanche Martin was once married to Cutter, whose real name it turned out was Christian Russo, then she knew plenty about mob behavior and actions. He had been dangerous, a murderer who himself murdered anyone he considered an enemy and ordered the killing of dozens during the mob wars. Many, many were never found.

Men like Cutter considered the mob their family.

Dick wondered *How involved Blanche, even Tess, had been with his family? What about now?*

Chapter 15

Mob Lawyers

Sitting in his favorite café on Madison Avenue in the Murray Hill District of NYC, a few blocks from the Mansion, Zero overheard all sorts of conversations.

Some humored him, others annoyed him. Mostly they fascinated him. People's lives, each different in some ways and so alike in others. The stories they were telling a person across from them, lies as well.

A woman sat down next to him. She began to perform a routine he had seen her perform many times before. First, she put on medical rubber gloves. Next, she wiped down the seat and arms of the chair, then the small table next to it where customers could set their drinks and papers. The café was known as a place a customer could sit for an hour or two. Some sat even longer.

After wiping down everything, she put a newspaper on the seat and started a conversation with Zero.

"Disgusting the type of people moving around here. Can you believe it?"

He didn't stay to listen. He wanted no conversation with this crazy lady. He decided to quietly get up, make no comment and move.

Zero was waiting for Dick. They usually loved to come here.

The colors of the walls were soothing, each a different shade of blue, the seats deep orange and rust tones. The people, mostly New Yorkers to the core were oblivious of others unless others annoyed them.

Many read the daily paper, having a four dollar cup of coffee with a fresh baked scone or muffin, and taking moments in time to watch people of all ages who came in. They came with their laptops, their iPads and their cell phones, reaching out all over the world.

Dick walked in, smiled, and waved. "Getting my coffee, darling?"

Zero laughed. A few people looked up, staring.

"Love you too, sweetie."

While waiting, Zero watched an elderly man. He read the paper, took short naps, and conversed if someone spoke to him, his walker and backpack sitting on the floor next to him. An employee told Zero he often stayed for hours and was there nearly every day. No one knew where he lived or much about him.

Except he smoked a lot. He would push his walker outside, no matter the weather. It was the kind with a seat. He would rest and smoke.

Dick yelled over from what had been a long line, "Dear, do you want anything?"

"No, sweetheart. Just you."

The two of them would do this for fun at a fancy restaurant or bar, much to Dora's annoyance.

At the table next to Zero sat a middle-aged couple, drinking their coffee quietly until the man looked up at the woman and said, "News was really depressing last night. Not much better in this morning's paper."

"I've given up on it. You know I only watch the weather reports now and hope I can find an old black & white film to watch, especially a murder mystery like *The Thin Man*, or *The Saint*. Too much ugliness going on everywhere it seems."

The man grimaced and replied, "Well, it's important to know what's happening."

"Why? I can't do anything about it."

"Good to be informed."

Nodding her head, she said, "I suppose."

It seemed to be her way of stopping him from pushing her to his way of thinking, as he probably had tried to do for years.

As Dick came to sit down, putting his coffee and roll on the table and taking off his winter jacket, they both heard someone standing in line go on and on about commercials on television.

"Really can you believe the drug companies? How they promote their garbage all for the love of more money? Use this drug and you'll feel wonderful again. Of course, in the background, someone is prancing in a field of flowers. Meantime a quiet voice reminds everyone listening that the side effects can include nausea, vomiting, stroke, heart attack, suicide and even death. Lovely!"

"Sounds like they don't appreciate the healthcare system in this country," Dick said, smirking.

"Plenty of people buy the Kool-Aid," Zero replied. He finished his coffee and waited for Dick to tell him why he wanted to meet so early.

The questions answered themselves.

She walked in.

It had been years since he'd seen her, but still there was no mistaking the stature of her body. Her hair was still a warm shade of light blond, and her face was graced with high cheek bones and deep grey eyes, almost black. Her eyes. That's what he remembered most about her.

Dick sat back, crossed his legs and gave a small nod to Zero when he realized he too recognized her, same as he had sitting in the café one morning a few days earlier.

"Remember, I asked if you wanted to meet me here after our card game? You went to bed. I needed some air, took a walk, and was as shocked as you seem to be."

Whispering, Zero said, "Dick, what the hell is she doing around here? She was an attorney for the mob when Socks was the witness against them."

"Right. Thankfully he had plenty of plastic surgery and doesn't look anything like he did when he testified."

Dick was busy watching to see if she did the same thing as the first time he saw her in this café.

Zero noticed it too. “She’s going behind the counter to the back of the café.”

“There’s about eight of these café’s. Four in the city, two in Brooklyn, Brooklyn Heights and Park Slope, and two on Long Island. They’re all close to the city in fact. I got curious.”

“Curious enough to do what?”

“See what her connection might be to the café.”

“And? Come on, Dick. What have you found out about her?”

“She and her family own all eight of these café’s.”

“Are you curious enough to talk to her?”

“Not yet. And do not tell Dora or she’ll be all over this place.”

Zero got up to get more coffee, leaned over and hugged Dick, to keep the dear and darling act going.

Dick kicked him in the leg, practically tripping him.

“Do be careful, dear.”

Zero leaned over Dick and patted him on the head. “Whatever you say, love.”

Dick watched for her to come back into the café.

Her name was Gina Torelli. She and her husband, Peter Torelli, had been attorneys for the mob. Dick remembered them all too clearly. They were mean, tough and didn’t take lightly to Socks turning witness for the prosecution. Having tried every legal maneuver to stop him from testifying, finally they had to admit defeat. Seeing her again after so many years, Dick recalled there were plenty of threats.

The Torelli's lived in Park Slope all their lives, now one of the most popular and expensive neighborhoods in the area, home to many Millennial and Generation X couples working their way up the ladder of money and power.

"Wasn't he murdered right after the trial?"

Zero had sat in the courtroom the last few days of the trial, listening to Dick and his associates ultimately win the case against a dangerous mob. They had terrorized too many people for too long and finally had been convicted and sent to prison. Many got life or worse, the death penalty.

Not something Dick agreed with then or now.

"He was. They found him about six months after the trial ended. He literally popped up in the bay. He had been stabbed to death."

Dick was taking out his cell phone, pretending to make a call, wanting to take a couple photos of her when she walked back into the café.

She had been in the back no more than ten minutes when she walked out with a box of what could be baked goods.

Dick clicked his phone then forwarded the photos to Detective Donnelly with a text message: *Remember her? Gina Torelli. Café on Madison near 38th*.

He responded *Holy s…t.*

Gina noticed them. She recognized Dick Zimmerman from the moment she saw him. His face was burned in her memory. Her husband was dead, murdered because he lost a case to him. Oh yes, she remembered him. She also remembered his annoying wife and that man with him.

It was her turn to send a message once she got into her dark sedan with dark tinted windows.

I have a job for you.

Chapter 16

After Dark

In the shadowy corners of the old meatpacking plant, no one would be able to hear him even if he could talk.

He was locked in a world of darkness, empty and lost.

The old plant had been replaced by a newer, larger, more efficient plant as this one became obsolete.

Vincent realized, like the place he was lost in, he no longer mattered. He was no longer of use to those who had ruled his life since early childhood. Those who had groomed him to be what it was they wanted. At first it was expected, later demanded.

Everything was blurred. Vague. Drugs were destroying his mind and body.

Love and affection were given when it pleased them. His life was exactly like the plant: cold, lonely and full of shadows following whatever he did.

In some ways, it was fine with him. He was tired. Even at his youthful age, he felt old and beaten by those demands and expectations.

The plant was a memory and a reminder of a dark world of criminal behavior, mob warfare and certainly murders. Soon his would be complete. He could hardly breathe as he stared at the black-and-white walls, blood-stained like the cement floor, darkened corners hiding decade old secrets.

Vincent realized no one could save him.

This plant was still owned by people who knew how to get rid of someone permanently.

He had known it when he saw them get out of the car in front of his apartment building.

Vincent left the door to his apartment unlocked. Why not? They would only break it down otherwise.

Waiting, he turned off his coffee maker, washed it and the one cup he used each day for his morning wakeup. His bed had been made neat. It always was. They had taught him about neatness and cleanliness being as important as their other expectations. Like loyalty and attention to detail, caution and avoiding being careless.

He had been careless and it was costing him his life. It wasn't that he so much forgot to turn off the front door alarm. He had been distracted by one of the residents asking a question about the damn holiday dinner. *Stupid question that time of night*, he thought.

"Vincent, we want to come in."

"The door is unlocked."

It was two men he had known since childhood. They too were doing only as they had been told by the people who were in charge.

"You have to come with us."

"I know."

"You could have run away somewhere."

"Where? They would find me."

"It's appreciated you didn't say anything to the police or the people snooping around where you worked."

"No matter. We're doing what's expected of us." Vincent put on his jacket and walked out with the two men, leaving behind his keys, wallet and cell phone. He wouldn't need them anymore.

V, he knew, had a key to his safety deposit box that held his will and a great deal of cash. He never told her how much he stashed away in case he needed it someday. Now she might.

"Please tell them how sorry I am."

"They know. So do we."

"Going to the plant?"

One of the two men sat in the back seat with him and nodded yes as the other drove them the short distance. He took out a syringe and stuck it in Vincent's neck. He would be dazed in minutes.

He felt them take him out of the car, walk him into a side door and tie him to a chair in a corner. They kept apologizing for having to do this. They had been friends, now they were his executioners.

Vincent would not be found for several days and an autopsy would reveal high doses of drugs in his system. Someone called to say he could be found in a car parked in a lower Manhattan parking garage. No name. No traceable phone.

Dr. Blythe Morrison was leaning over the body and pulled the sheet back. "See the puncture mark in his neck? We've done a toxicology screening. Vincent had excessive amounts of cocaine in his system. Enough injected into him to kill a horse. Same drug we found in Romero."

Detective Donnelly and the Zimms were standing over the body as she pointed to the mark. They were at the chief medical examiner building on First Avenue.

"These murders must be connected. Detective, how did you find him?"

"Got an anonymous tip from a burner phone."

"Has anyone claimed the body?" Dick asked.

"Not yet. Chances are no one will. They'll be too scared."

"Have you found out who owns the garage where he was found?"

Dora leaned over the body of this poor young soul, murdered for what reason they had no idea.

"My sergeant is checking on it. They have crime scene tape around the building and they're looking for the owner. Chances are it won't matter. He most likely was just dumped there after he was killed ."

Dr. Morrison startled them by saying, "By the way, we found something strange scratched on the palms of his hands."

Dora, Dick and Detective Donnelly stared at them. He had the letter V scratched into one hand; the other had a question mark.

"What is V?"

It was of course who was V.

New power struggles now faced the family.

Mistakes had been made, forcing them to order two murders.

Now they ordered hits on those investigating them and on V. They feared exposure ending their dangerous secret society.

Chapter 17

Witness

As their grip on Manhattan tightened, competition between the mobs continued until there was an outright war. Members were gunned down in the streets of Manhattan, Brooklyn, the Bronx and out to Long Island.

There had been gangs and gang wars in New York since the 1850s with names like The Dead Rabbits, The Daybreak Boys, The Bowery Boys, The Eastman Gang, and The Forty Thieves. They were made up mostly of men, although on occasion a woman joined them. Equally cruel and violent.

As some gangs were eliminated, others sprung up. The fear they created caused bloody riots between the gangs and in the communities they terrorized. There was just so much money to be made. The fight for power denied rational behavior.

The lure of the money and control motivated their attitudes and actions usually fed on by psychopathic egos. By the mid 1950's the gangs had become more sophisticated, more complex and consequently, more dangerous and deadly.

The police, fortunately, also had newer and better investigative methods, stronger forensic tools and an increase in their numbers. Ultimately most of the mob gangs were wiped out by their own violence toward each other and police ramping up their surveillance and ultimately arrests. There were a few like Socks willing to give testimony against them and enter the Witness Protection Program. Some gang members swore to have their revenge someday.

Socks was concerned this might be that day.

He told Dick with angst in his voice, "I knew these people and how they behaved. They could wait years before retaliating. We have to be careful, very careful. They probably have people watching out for them that you would never suspect."

"You need to stay out of this. Take your walks. Stay in touch with me by phone."

Socks had hated living away from Manhattan. Once he returned he would take long walks, often taking photos, sometimes sitting at an outdoor café watching New Yorkers and tourists move up and down the streets, in and out of shops and restaurants.

He loved walks around the city's ethnic areas. Chinatown, with ducks hanging in many restaurant windows, and Little Italy, stopping in one of its famous bakeries. Over to Delancey and Orchard Streets where there used to be pushcarts in the once primarily Jewish neighborhood including Henry Street, known now as the Henry Street Settlement.

Sometimes he walked uptown on Fifth Avenue toward Central Park where the mansions of the wealthy once bordered its landscape. At one time the park was home to freed African Americans and other residents who had set up small communities, only to be displaced in order to create what was to become the more than 800-acre park. There had been years of changes, political infighting and decline before Robert Moses took over care of that valuable piece of land bringing it to its present day beauty and recreational use for New Yorkers who could find an escape from their small apartments and crowded city life.

So many people came to America. While thousands would settle westward, there were those who found New York the center of their universe. They too would spread out, to Staten Island, Queens, the Bronx and Brooklyn and eventually east on Long Island.

All religions. All people.

They came across the ocean, strangers arriving in a land promising hope and a better way of life. For many it was. For many others it was not. Some of them found their security and opportunity in gangs.

There was power in numbers. They felt connected and supported. They were willing to fight for their piece of the American Dream. Some were willing to steal, harm and kill for it.

"By the way, what did you know about Alphonse?" Dick asked. "You saw his photo in the paper."

"I saw Alphonse and his boyfriend in the neighborhood sometimes. They were walking, holding hands, sitting at one of the bars, listening to the sweet sounds of jazz flowing out of the clubs onto the streets on warm evenings."

It was true New York.

"I also saw him talking once to the girl I followed running out of the Mansion the night he was killed. The girl whose photo I took and showed to you. She was hiding by the entrance of the Mansion and ran away when the alarm went off."

It was seeing Blanche Martin after all these years that sent him in a tail- spin until he spoke with Dick again.

That's when he told him.

How could he forget?

Frankie Socks remembered what it was like growing up in his neighborhood, where the people were mostly poor or poorer, except for the mob. When his brother promised him a way to make money, to have a sense of belonging, it was hard to refuse. Because if you refused, your family could be hurt. The mob was in control. They didn't just make threats. They acted on them.

"He was my brother. He warned me not to say no," Socks explained. "They own this part of town. They own everyone and everything that matters. Store owners who say no could soon have their businesses burned down. Sometimes even worse."

"How old were you when you started with them?"

"The first time. I was fourteen. They gave me a box, said not to open it and just deliver it to some store owner. Fifteen minutes after I walked away the store blew up. From then on, I did whatever they asked of me."

"Like what?"

"Sometimes deliver a package like the first one. As I got older they had me pick up envelopes and bring them back to the club where they hung out. Gave me a large brown envelope to put them in. I knew they were payoffs. I never opened one, never took anything from them. I didn't want any, plus I knew better. Some guy did that once and they cut off his hand."

"When did you start driving for them?"

"Cutter asked for me. My brother told him he could trust me. Two weeks after that my brother was killed in an auto accident. For some reason they decided they needed to get rid of him. I never knew why. I overheard talk, mostly they felt he was a liability for some reason."

"Did you ever question them about it?"

"Never. They said how horrible it was that it happened. They paid for the funeral. Said I should let them know if I ever needed anything. I wanted to get even with them. Never forgave them for killing him."

"Is that why you agreed to testify against them?"

"Yes. And I wanted out."

"Did you drive Cutter many times?"

"Sure, for several years. That's how I met Blanche. He would have me drive them out to Brooklyn or the Bronx where they would go for dinner or have clandestine meetings. I waited in the car and I listened. All the time I listened. I paid attention to who they met, who they planned to kill, how they planned to expand their territory."

"What was she like?"

"Blanche?"

"Yeah, her."

"She could be real nasty. If she wanted someone to disappear they did."

"In your testimony you said you were sure Cutter was not head of the mob even though he always claimed he was."

"One time, I overheard Cutter and Blanche talking. There was a lot of traffic driving over the Brooklyn Bridge into Manhattan; they probably figured I was too occupied to pay any attention to them.

"He told her, 'The boss wants us to expand it east. I'm not sure it's a good idea. It would be difficult to control. Divides up our people resources too much, easy to lose control of what everyone is doing.'"

"Sounds like she was very involved in mob activities."

"She was. I often heard her making suggestions to Cutter. He asked her if there was any way she thought it could work."

"Diamonds and drugs. North Shore of Long Island in Nassau County is wealthy. The husbands love the drugs especially the ones who work on Wall Street."

"Did you ever have a problem with her?"

"Are you kidding? I was very careful around her. I thought she was worse than he was."

Socks remembered how Dick had explained it all to him when he offered to place him in witness protection.

"It's offered by the justice system before and after any testimony you would give against the Cutter Crime Family. You'll be provided with a new identify, a place to live and you'll be protected by the government. They won't be able to find or hurt you."

"Where would I go?"

"I'm not sure. That will all be worked out once you agree to testify."

That had been over twenty years ago and here he was once again, most unexpectedly facing that enemy. Everyone thought they no longer existed in any way.

But they did.

Chapter 18

Mickey's

Mickey's had a huge tree in the window with shiny silver bells and colored lights blinking on and off.

Next to it was a tall menorah with blue and white candles.

"I'm an equal opportunity celebrator," Mickey had told Dick and Dora.

The place was crowded, filled with people in a holiday mood. Meaning a whole lot of food, drinks and partying. In some places in the city it got out of control. Rarely at Mickey's. His patrons kept it civilized.

This night the only thing that seemed out of control was the murders of Alphonse and Vincent.

Carson picked up his scotch and water, took a healthy drink, and then suggested, "Maybe those two ladies have some relatives you could talk to about them."

"We will once you get us names of those relatives." Dick glared at him.

"Hey, I just got into this. You'll have it. I have one of my best researchers on it."

Dora put her arm around Dick, whispered something in his ear and with a grin called the waiter over to order dinner. He laughed. They both did. She knew how to calm him down.

"I agree. They're acting very suspicious. Carson, you keep checking through the media. I have people in the police department checking old records. Once you get your information we'll put that in our system too and compare what we have."

Donnelly had joined them. He was a stickler for details, part of what made him good at what he did. Donnelly loved to hang out in his cousin Mickey's bar. They were more than cousins, they were friends.

Dick and Dora and Zero and many others over the years heard the Donnelly's story. Nature of owning a bar, people love to hear stories after a drink or two or three…or more.

"Once when we were young boys around nine, we had been proving we could walk across ice in a park near our house. Shawn sunk into a melted patch of ice screaming for help. I ran and pulled him out, and we're lucky we both didn't sink into that section of the ice. Freezing we dragged ourselves home to not too pleased parents."

That day cemented a lifelong friendship.

A darn good thing to have in a city like Manhattan.

"When we were eighteen, we went to NYU, moved in together and over the years decided on different careers. For Shawn it was a stint in the Navy, followed by law enforcement. Mickey was 4F due to bad eyesight. Yet, even as our lives and careers changed, our affection and support for each other did not."

A patron would often ask, "You and Shawn both get married?"

"I did, had a couple kids, and live in the same neighborhood where I grew up right over the Brooklyn Bridge. Shawn never married. That's where we differ. He's lived most of his adult life in a loft apartment in SOHO. He became a city cop, then a city detective. He was happy to be Uncle Shawn to my kids."

"Kids, a house with a mortgage, in-laws, not for me," Shawn always told anyone who asked. Over the years Dick and Dora had eaten often at Mickey's. Sometimes Shawn or Zero, even Carson joined them. Sometimes others from the Mansion did too. Especially for any celebration and reason to raise a few toasts.

Dora, Zero, Shawn and Carson listened as Dick told them about his recent conversations with Socks and then Vincent, including his admission that he had killed Alphonse Romero.

This night, the voices in Mickey's seemed to disappear into a dark cloud of murder so close by.

Their senses shouted much more violence was about to happen.

Chapter 19

In The News

"Dick, hope you're ready for me to blow your minds. We all need to meet, five P.M. today."

"Okay, Carson. Meet at our place, it's more private."

At three thirty, Dora ordered drinks and appetizers from Mickey's set to arrive at four forty-five.

There was an expensive red wine and several platters of food. The Zimms were always generous. It didn't matter if it was a meeting or a party. Most likely why people didn't turn down an invitation from them. Plus they were really fun.

This was no party.

The look on Carson's face made it obvious he found some unexpected information on the Martin sisters.

Setting up his laptop on their white oak dining room table, he inserted a flash drive. They waited for him to be ready. Zero was shrugging his shoulders, Donnelly picked up some food and Dick and Dora glanced at each other, wondering what was going on.

The screen on the computer showed several newspaper articles from a little over ten years earlier.

Next to one of them was a photo of a man, maybe early thirties at the time. Even in the black=and-white photo it seemed as if his eyes looked right through you.

"His name is Mario Russo."

There was a small tattoo of a tiny knife on the left side of his neck.

Dick immediately knew he was related to Cutter. He stepped back, put his arm around Dora.

"Carson, is he still in jail?"

"Yes. I called and checked."

"Who is he?"

Zero poured himself a second glass of wine and sat back down on the living room sofa, waiting for an answer.

"Mario Russo is Blanche and Cutter's son. Cutter's name was originally Christian Russo. He later changed it to Martin, his mother's maiden name. Cutter and Mario have the same tattoo.

Blanche used the name Martin. For some reason Tess took it too.

"She never took her second husband's last name?" Zero asked.

"Nope. Never did that. She married him to go into hiding, if you ask me."

They all looked at Dick who was standing by the window with a drink in his hand as Dora moved away to look closer at the photo.

"Remember, I prosecuted him. I arranged witness testimony against him and others in his mob."

"Carson, what else is there on this Mario?"

"Dick, it gets better."

"I followed the story back to his arrest and called a Fed source I have. He owed me a favor. Seems like Mario is being used as an informant."

"An informant for what?" Dora asked as Carson scrolled down on some other articles he had for them.

"Apparently some of the original Cutter mob created a secret crime organization called Drugs for Diamonds. We've been aware of it for a while but have never been able to get to them."

Donnelly so far had ignored the information about Mario being an informant. But it got Zero's attention.

"You mean like Murder, Incorporated was in the 1930's and 1940's?" Zero had known a few of that crowd, but it wasn't something he bragged about.

"Wait a minute, they killed a hell of a lot of people. Is that happening with this group?"

"Murder, Inc. was a group of Italian mafia and Jewish mobsters in different neighborhoods of Brooklyn, the Bronx and Manhattan. Reports claimed they were responsible for hundreds of killings until they were finally caught. Many were sent to prison, others executed."

"Damn if I really know. I have one of my researchers checking out other sources."

"Carson, what prison is Mario in?" Zero looked up from his wine and food now listening to every word.

"Nearby. Sing Sing, upstate New York."

"I called. They wouldn't give me a list of his visitors or phone calls over the phone. They needed a request from the police."

"If Blanche is related, she must visit or call him. Wouldn't you think?"

"Dick, how about you, Carson and I make a visit to Sing Sing tomorrow and find out what and who this guy knows," Donnelly said, getting on his phone calling the prison.

"I'll let them know we're coming and want to visit with this guy," he said.

He had known Mario was a confidential informant. It didn't get him out of jail. Now, it did get him better privileges and an opportunity to get out of jail before he was an old man.

There was much more to his story.

They would find out soon enough. Talk about devious behavior and dysfunctional families.

Dora had an idea of her own she wanted to check out.

She would need Zero's help. How could he possibly say no to Lady D? Dick would kill him if any harm came to her.

Chapter 20

Sing Sing Correctional Facility

The ride outside of the city, up north on FDR drive over to the Taconic Parkway changes scenery from city to rural with a few farms along the country roads. Ultimately they took the road off to Ossining, New York.

The landscape of the area, try as hard as it had is still enveloped by the site of the looming maximum security prison, 30 miles north of New York City and on the banks of the Hudson River where hundreds had been executed by the electric chair.

"They are no longer allowed to do executions here." Dick began reading some information to them as they took the drive up to meet with Mario.

"At one time, the A.C.L.U. declared and I do quote, 'The death penalty violates the constitutional ban against cruel and unusual punishment and the guarantees of due process of law and of equal protection under the law. Furthermore, we believe that the state should not give itself the right to kill human beings—especially when it kills with premeditation and ceremony, in the name of the law or in the name of its people, and when it does so in an arbitrary and discriminatory fashion.'"

Donnelly drove as Dick read about Sing Sing Prison.

"Listen to this. In 1972 the death penalty was declared unconstitutional, 'if application was inconsistent and arbitrary.' Since that time a majority of states passed their own death penalty laws."

Carson sitting in the back was making notes. The whole situation would prove to be one hell of a story.

Trying to change the subject, Donnelly told them, "My sergeant's made an appointment for us with the warden and to meet with Mario Russo."

"Good, hope he can give us some insight into all this. Amazing, here we are on the road where hundreds of visitors to Sing Sing traveled over dozens of years. Has to be a road paved with anger and grief, frustration and despair for so many people."

"Dick, It's hard to accept how people let their lives disintegrate into such ugliness," Donnelly answered, driving towards the entrance to the huge stone structure that kept people locked in for years, some a lifetime.

"I know. Yet every time I helped send someone here I felt they could have been saved at one time in their life."

"Wishful thinking," Donnelly replied. "Some people have what I always called a mean gene. Got that way young and kept it all their life, only got meaner and meaner, some becoming killers."

The entrance to the prison fit the fortress they were entering, each step bleak and almost smothering with its cement walls and huge doors locked shut. They kept prisoners from fleeing. *They also keep out hope*, Dick thought as the three of them were escorted to their meeting.

The warden was surprisingly pleasant looking and had a kind manner that belied the life he led in this dark place.

They had agreed on the ride up that Donnelly would ask the questions and make it as professional as possible, a police investigation.

"We would like information on your inmate, Mario Russo," he said. "Need to know who has visited him, when and how often? Who has called him? Who has he called? We also need to speak with him."

The warden nodded, made a call and turned leading them through the grey stone jungle.

Handcuffed and wearing ankle shackles, Mario was brought to the phone room, only a glass wall between them. Guards stood on both sides of the wall.

He had been in Sing Sing for over ten years, now in his early forties, hair thinning and walking with a limp. His eyes hard as steel, he stared at all three of the men.

"I'm Detective Donnelly. The warden said you agreed to talk to us. We have some questions if that's okay with you?"

Neither Donnelly nor Mario showed any recognition of each other. His staying alive as a confidential informant depended on such discretion.

"Like what questions? I don't get out much," he said his grin matching the steel in his eyes. His voice still maintained a Brooklyn accent. The small knife tattoo, same as Cutter's, marred the side of his neck.

"We've been told the man known as Cutter was your father?"

"Yeah, that was my old man."

"Your mother, Blanche? And Tess, your aunt?"

"Right again. So if you know all this what don't you know?"

Mario was smoking, making the glass between them fog up. A clock on the wall behind him ticked away time. Time is what the inmates had plenty of. He was prolonging their time together. The longer it went the more time he had out of his small and confining prison cell.

"Mario, we've been told Blanche visits you a few times a year. You've also had some visits over the years from a Vincent Blair."

Vincent's name caused Mario to squirm in his hard white plastic chair. The prison guard standing behind him watched his movements, body rigid in anticipation.

"Sure, knew him back in the day. A close buddy."

"How close a buddy?"

Donnelly could feel him shutting down. Mario had turned to look at the guard as if telling him they're done.

Mario suddenly glanced up at Dick.

"Hey. I know you. Saw pictures of you. You got Cutter sent away for life. Got a few of his pals sent away too. Why are you here?"

"I knew your buddy Vincent." Dick said the word "buddy" softly.

"What the hell does that mean?"

"He's been murdered."

Mario, clearly upset, began to sit up after lighting another cigarette. His right eye twitching, he turned back to Donnelly. "I don't wanna talk anymore today."

Donnelly knew saying today was a clue, a hint, he was giving him that he had more to tell him in confidence. That would come.

Carson had been writing the whole time. He realized there was much more to this story.

How was everyone really related? Why did Blanche visit him? How did Mario and Vincent really know each other?

The truth would stun them.

Chapter 21

In Harm's Way

Two people murdered.

The men who had followed Dick and Dora into Chinatown would show themselves again intent on harming them.

Impatient. That was Dora. When she wanted something it often meant—now.

"I want to look again for those photos you saw in the Martin sister's bedroom."

"How do you propose to do that? Those two have hardly left here since the murder."

"Zero, dearest."

"Oh, oh, Lady D, I don't like the way this sounds."

They were having coffee in the Mansion dining room, Dora suggesting her plan for lunchtime. "You keep an eye on the sisters. I'll ask Bertie to keep them distracted."

"What if they get up to leave?"

"Improvise. Trip one of them."

A little after noon, Bertie sat down to chat with the sisters. As soon as she did, Dora raced to the sisters' condo.

Socks came in through the back entrance, went up the rear elevator and met her to unlock their door, a skill he had mastered years ago.

Dora went through the dresser drawers. No photos.

The place was different since they had found the body.

"I can't find any photos and their condo looks different. For one thing the second bedroom where the body was found has been stripped of all bedding and the drawers are empty. I think they're planning to leave this place."

"Hopefully, they are going to move," Socks replied, locking the door behind them.

"Maybe. Sure isn't right."

They got on the back elevator, Socks not wanting to take any chance of being seen by the sisters.

On the first floor, it opened to the two men who had followed her and Dick to Chinatown.

"Grab her," one of them yelled, pulling Dora out of the elevator.

Socks kicked him and pulled Dora close to him.

"I got him. I said grab her." The other man started to tackle Socks as Dora screamed at them.

"What are you doing here? What do you want?"

Zero who had been on alert, heard her screams and ran from the lunchroom. He knew she had gone up the back elevator.

Zero ran down the hall and saw Dora and Socks fighting the two men.

Distracted by the sight of another man coming at them gave Socks a chance to take aim and hit a solid punch to his target.

"Get off me, you nutcase," Dora shouted and bit the other man, still trying to drag her out of the building.

Zero came up behind him, threw him on the floor, kicked him in the groin, and knocked him moaning to the ground. Dora went flying out of his arms and on to the ground, more annoyed than hurt.

All this happened within minutes, and before the police could be called.

Realizing they better get out of there, the two men, one limping, raced out the back door into a waiting black sedan driving off into the busy city streets.

"Who the hell are those guys?" Zero helped Dora up, making sure she was okay.

Socks was on the floor catching his breath. It had been a long time since he had done battle of any sort.

"They look like the ones who followed Dick and me the other night." Grinning, she showed them a chunk of hair she pulled from the guy who grabbed her.

"Maybe police forensics can identify him from this."

"Think the sisters had them waiting here?"

"Socks, they probably have some type of alarm in their place to warn if there's any intruders. Must be why they were waiting for us."

"Let's go over to Mickey's. I need a drink," Zero said. "I don't care what time it is. We'll call Donnelly from there." Zero threw his jacket around Dora's shoulders, put his arm through hers and out they went, leaving Socks to gratefully disappear from the Mansion.

All settled into their booth, Zero called Donnelly.

"He's sending over one of his officers to stand guard here," he told Dora after hanging up.

"Did he say when they would be back?"

"He and Dick want to meet us at the police station around four o'clock to look at some mug shots. They're still upstate at Sing Sing."

"I don't know which of you I'm more furious with for pulling this stunt. We're dealing with some seriously bad people who enjoy killing." Donnelly paced the room. Dick sat quietly. Dora wasn't sure which was worse.

Dick's quiet was not good for Dora. Only when he was really upset with her was he that quiet.

"Okay, dear, I know you're upset with me. It's just that we wanted to see if we could find the photos Zero saw the other night."

"I could have gotten a search warrant," Donnelly told her, quite emphatically.

Dora was rubbing her arm, only slightly bruised from where she had been grabbed. Zero was leaning back on a chair in the police station. Socks had ran off. No police or police station for him he told Dora and Zero.

"I'm sorry, really I am. I realize I put all three of us in harm's way." Dora was upset for upsetting Dick.

It would be after nine when they got home. Dick poured himself a drink, and sat on his favorite chair starring out at the holiday lights flashing through the windows. Their inside low lighting caused shadows to splash across the wall behind him, making it look as if monsters were dancing across their room.

"Don't you realize I would be devastated if anything happened to you?"

"Yes."

"You can't go off like this, as if you're some good looking Ms. Marple."

Dora couldn't help but smile. "I know. I know. But…"

"There shouldn't be any but…"

"Shawn is furious with all of you. No more sleuthing around on your own like you did today. Promise me."

"Promise." Dora nodded her head yes.

Her fingers were crossed behind her back.

"I'm going to bed."

"Donnelly has a tip on where to find V," Dick said. "I want to be there when he brings her in for questioning."

Dora went over, gave Dick a hug, and pulled him from the chair, all the time wondering, *What story do those missing photos tell*?

Chapter 22

Family Ties

There are many kinds of families.

My Three Sons. Ozzie and Harriett. Leave it To Beaver. All made up, almost mythical television families sending messages of how to be the perfect family. Rules most people couldn't live by.

Not in real life.

In real life families were connected through blood relatives and blood promises.

Cutter and Blanche's family was connected through demands and expectations and ultimately the consequences of their actions.

Many of their family ties were lost because of gang war murders. Others due to arrests or being driven underground. A new type of criminal had begun to emerge after that. White-collar crimes surfaced from Wall Street to Madison Avenue, and across the country in big and small cities alike.

The players were offering insider trading, some selling worthless stocks, others perpetuating Ponzi schemes. There were bankers doing illegal mortgage lending to unsuspecting people looking for their dream home. There were and still are plenty of crooked businessman, politicians, and more.

Zero and the Zimms were having dinner at Mickey's. The earlier light snow turned to heavy snowflakes and suddenly sidewalks needed shoveling. Inside Mickey's, it was warm and welcoming.

"Money," said Zero.

"It's been all about money and power playing host to their egos. Buy that expensive car, build a bigger house, travel abroad and enjoy those drugs. Lots and lots of drugs."

"We had people coming to my law firm before I retired," Dick added, "They had been conned out of their savings, cheated for one reason or another."

"The Wall Street money managers made a fortune, and put plenty of it into drugs and lots of free, crazy sex. They used hundred dollar bills to snort their coke."

Dora let Dick and Zero talk, all the time, considering how some family ties can be tragic and disastrous. She had seen it many times as a judge in divorce court. But something else was bothering her.

"Gentleman."

They knew to listen. Dora never called them gentleman unless she had something very serious to ask them or talk to them about.

"Has anyone claimed Vincent's body?"

There was a moment of silence, each looking rather quizzically at the other shaking their heads no.

"Not yet. According to Donnelly there were a couple calls about him that couldn't be traced. People asking where he was going to be buried."

Dick leaned forward on his elbows, not wanting to be overheard telling Zero and Dora about the meeting with Mario Russo.

"He knows a lot more. I doubt he's just a buddy, which is what he claimed."

"Carson checking on it?"

"Yeah. Donnelly too. Dr. Morrison's people are working on forensics to see what they can find."

"Damn strange."

"Speaking of strange, Zero, your tie is blinking and causing a stir at the bar with that blonde."

Zero laughed, sent her a drink and stood up to go over to introduce himself. Dressed for attention for the holidays he wore his bow tie that blinked red and green, and a red shirt. He also made sure they saw he had on one green sock and one red one.

Grinning at Zero, Dick said, "Well, Santa's helper, your socks remind me I need to be in touch with Frankie Socks."

"Glad to be of help, my dear man."

Like a lot of romantic relationships for Zero, the lady at the bar would be fun company, although short lived. An hour or two at the bar was enough for him. He had a lot of good memories and that suited him fine.

Before they left, Dora asked, "Who is Vincent's family? Where are they?"

Dick looked at his wife, "Sweetheart, we simply don't know. Yet."

Chapter 23

Rabbi Feldman and a Different Kind of Family

The Zimms were in New York this time of year because the synagogue was honoring Zero. Dora and Dick had met with the rabbi the previous spring and recommended he receive their annual Humanitarian Award.

The synagogue had accepted his money for many years even though they knew he had some shady business dealings at times. The donations amounted to several million dollars and had been distributed at the rabbi's discretion with the understanding it was to help people, not for building upkeep.

Zero had a great deal of money left to him many years ago by a family member. It had been sent to him, to hold, or keep as it turned out, if they did not escape the terrors in Germany against the Jewish people.

He had never spent any of it on himself, even when his business went bad, even when he was nearly broke for a brief time.

Zero met Rabbi Feldman through Dora even before she married Dick. Every so often he would go to synagogue with her and her family.

Over the years he visited the rabbi, having conversations with him about religion, philosophy and of course politics.

"Rabbi, I agree with you on some points of view, not on others."

"We do agree it can be an unjust world."

"What about God, Rabbi?" They disagreed on viewpoints of God.

"Zero, why have you donated so much to the synagogue," the rabbi once asked him.

"In response to those who committed horrible acts on the Jewish people."

"So Tikkun Olam?"

"Yes."

"I assume you see these as acts of charity to help repair the world and pursue social justice." The rabbi understood Zero. He was a kind man who felt grateful for the good in his life, letting go of regrets. Holding on to them did no one any good. He and the rabbi had conversations over the years on many issues. Regrets. Excuses. Forgiveness. Friendship. Love. Human frailty.

Zero smiled. He trusted this man. He trusted him to do the right thing with the money, to give it where it mattered, where it would do the most good.

Rabbi Feldman truly liked Zero. He appreciated his donations and agreed with Dora. "Yes, we should thank him."

Dora was sitting with the rabbi, planning the evening and discussing how to get the unsuspecting Zero to the synagogue the following week and to be sure he was dressed in a normal tuxedo. Not one with a blinking tie. It was not going to be easy.

"Hey, at my age, I can be free to be silly," he'd say.

That would not work for the award evening, a catered, first class, black tie event held in beautiful surroundings. This year it would be in one of the synagogue's major benefactors huge and fabulous Fifth Avenue apartment that took up one whole floor of the building facing the Metropolitan Museum of Art.

Wearing a long, dark green wool coat with matching slacks, white cashmere turtle neck sweater, her hair pulled back and small gold hoop earrings, the rabbi marveled at how much younger Dora looked than her actual age.

"You look wonderful, Dora, almost younger each year."

"You're just a big flirt, Rabbi." She grinned, knowing he meant the compliment.

She and Rabbi Feldman had known each other since she was a young girl. He was in awe of her aging with so much grace and charm. He was not aging as gracefully. He felt tired more easily and thought maybe it was time for him to retire. He loved what he did. The synagogue was an important family to him, as much as his wife and children and grandchildren.

Dora smiled at him. “We’ll figure out how to get him here. I’ll tell him Dick is being honored. He won’t refuse to come for that. I hope.”

It was scheduled for the Sunday after Thanksgiving.

Thanksgiving was tomorrow.

A lot could happen before then.

Chapter 24

V

"I only brought messages to Vincent."

"What kind of messages?"

"Information."

"Fine. What kind of information?"

This back and forth between V and Detective Donnelly had been going on for over two hours. They had found V hiding out in Vincent's apartment where she screamed and cursed at them as they entered and finally arrested her for pushing and kicking one of the officers.

More like punched him and tried to escape out the window down a fire escape.

Dick was observing the interview from the other side of the interrogation room window.

She knows what happened to Alphonse and Vincent, he thought.

Soon they would learn she was related by family ties and bound by family values and excessive demands.

Surveillance had been kept on Vincent's apartment and when she showed up, the police called Detective Donnelly and they had her. They had hoped for this. She was their only real lead to the two murders and much more.

They had no idea how convoluted it would turn out to be.

"Let's start with your full name. What does V stand for?"

Detective Donnelly finally got her to calm down, mostly through her own sheer exhaustion and she responded with little emotion.

"Valentina."

"Valentina what?"

"Valentina Blair. Vincent is my older brother by two years. I've been called V since I was two. Family said I couldn't pronounce my name."

"Vincent's been murdered."

"I know. That's why I went to his apartment."

"How did you know? Who killed him? And enough with the snippy answers."

"Word gets around, that's how I know."

"Tell me about the messages you would bring to him."

"No."

"Are you afraid of someone?"

"Aren't you the clever detective?"

"Who are you afraid of? We can help you."

V laughed, leaned back, stretched her long legs out in front of her, and faced the detective. "I want my lawyer."

"My sergeant called the number you gave us to request your attorney. They said they were not available at this time."

V sat stoic. That was a message. She knew that meant they planned to kill her too.

"What were you looking for in his apartment?"

Silence.

"Put her in a cell. Charge her with resisting arrest and assaulting a police officer. We'll see if her attorney shows up."

She knew someone acting as an attorney would come for her. Outside waiting would be the same two men who killed Vincent. Alone in a dark cell, V realized if she talked to the detective she might survive.

Banging on the cell bars, V screamed, "I want to talk to the detective. Tell him I know who killed Alphonse and Vincent. I know why."

Dick had left knowing there was nothing more he could do here. He wanted to check on Dora.

It was after midnight when V heard footsteps on the concrete floor walking toward her.

Chapter 25

Conversation with Dick

He looked familiar.

The elderly man was surely over eighty. He stooped and had only a few grey hairs left springing up from his balding head. Age spots covered his face and hands.

It was his eyes. The soul of this man was in his eyes.

It took Dick a while to remember where he had seen them before, who they belonged to.

The man who rarely stayed at this condo got off the elevator at the same time as Dick. They were both startled for the moment. The Zimms penthouse condo was to the right; the other man's was to the left. They had never actually met.

Dick recognized the man's grin.

He knew who he was.

Dick waited a short time then knocked on his door.

"Can we talk?"

"Of course. What's happened?"

Sitting down in a worn beige leather chair with deep cushions, Dick was appreciative for the opportunity to talk about what was happening to someone he believed could be totally impartial and offer some insights.

The other man sat in a matching chair. Each held a glass of scotch. A full bottle sat on a side table ready for refills.

"It began with the murder of Alphonse Romero, a tango instructor found in bed at the Martin sisters' condo here at the Mansion. There's also been another murder, Vincent Blair, the night manager here. Now a couple of men, probably hit men, are after Dora and me."

"How much is known about the murders?"

"Carson Gladstone, a city reporter, has a friend on the paper helping him do research on the Martin sisters, way back twenty to thirty years. He found out Blanche Martin was married to the head of the Cutter Crime Family."

"Oh!"

"You've heard of him?"

"Very dangerous man."

"I was one of the attorneys responsible for putting him away for life. He died in prison a number of years ago."

"I'm surprised he didn't get the death penalty."

"Yeah. Well he finally turned over some information on others in his mob and his sentence was reduced to life."

"Am I correct that they actually couldn't execute any longer?"

"True, not since 2004."."

"What about the men following you and your wife? Could you identify them?"

"Dora got a better look at them when they tried to grab her off the elevator. Said they were wearing dark baseball jackets and caps."

"Do the police know about them?"

"Sure. Detective Donnelly is a good man and a friend for many years. I'm worried we are missing something, but not sure what."

Dick got up to refill both of their glasses with the expensive scotch and stood looking around the room. There was a lifetime of memories in photos on the man's walls and tables.

"Great photos, aren't they?"

"You have plenty of your own stories."

"Many, yes." Leaning back in the chair, he waited for Dick to continue.

"Mind if I pace around a bit? Sometimes it helps me think better."

"Sometimes a cigarette does that for me."

"Feel free. I gave them up many years ago but still have moments of wanting one."

"Dick, what's bothering you the most?"

"My concern for Dora. She goes off investigating without fear, leaving me to have enough fear for both of us. And of course they might actually kill one or both of us."

"Who are you suspicious of the most?"

"Blanche Martin. Maybe her sister too."

"You need to go visit where they used to live. It's possible they own homes and other property there."

"Which could also mean they still have connections from the past when Blanche was married to Cutter."

"That could mean anyone."

"Certainly does."

"Do you miss your work?"

"Sometimes, but as you can see, my memories are very much with me."

"Will you join us for Thanksgiving dinner tomorrow?"

"No. I prefer my privacy. You can visit again if you like. The murders fascinate me."

Chapter 26

One Down

"Terminate her."

Detective Donnelly got a call from Mario Russo. "V is to be terminated."

"By who?"

"Someone acting as her attorney, or they'll try to sneak in late at night. You can stop them. I need you to do that for me."

"Of course."

The detective called his sergeant and two officers into his office and told them about V and made his plan to protect her.

"I want one of you officers in the cells on each side of her cell. We can make the cells appear locked. The sergeant and I will be on the other side of the door. We'll have a camera set up watching all the movements back there."

Donnelly went to tell V what was happening. It was getting colder and she was shivering.

"I'll get you another blanket. The officers will be here all night. We're watching for any possibility. We expect they'll try to come in through a back entrance which is usually locked and has an alarm."

"It won't stop them."

"We don't want it to. We want to capture and arrest them."

"They'll come armed."

"We will be too."

V and the officers in the cells next to her heard the late night footsteps approaching. They made no effort to wear shoes that made no noise. The sound on the concrete floors like thunder, each step they took put everyone on alert.

There were so many shadows in the cells caused by their flashlights, the men preparing to do what they had been instructed, intending to terminate V and leave the same way they came. A car was waiting for them.

There were ten cells. Only three of them had anyone in them. Others in holding cells had been removed earlier unaware of what was happening.

Donnelly saw the men break into the back entrance after disarming the alarm. They were dressed all in black including black ski masks.

Whispering to his sergeant, he said, "Here they come. Let the officers in the cells know to be ready and be sure V is at the back of her cell looking like she's asleep."

The sound of the footsteps got closer to V's cell. The two men had glanced in each cell they passed with their flashlight. The officers next to V also acted as if they were sound sleep. One even did a great imitation of a loud snore.

When they heard one of the men say "There she is," all hell broke loose.

Donnelly began to shout to his sergeant who came in from the station's main room. The two officers jumped out of their cells at the same time and tackled the men with guns intent on killing V. She stayed in a far corner of her cell, still shivering, now mostly from fear.

"Stay where you are. Don't move. You're under arrest."

The taller of the two fired at one of the officers. Donnelly shot him dead, right through the heart. The other man was tangling with the sergeant and second officer and with one final punch he was laid out on the cement floor. Then handcuffed and thrown into one of the cells.

"V, hurry up, we need to leave right now."

She was given a heavy winter coat with a hood and quickly taken to a pre-arranged safe house where officers would protect her in twelve-hour shifts.

The sergeant checked out the back door where the men had entered. The driver of the car waiting for the two hit men must have heard the gunshots and drove quickly away.

They were already slipping into the busy city traffic.

Over the next couple days, the surviving hit man would be questioned at length. All he did was continue to say, "I want a lawyer."

None ever came. Same as with V.

For his protection they quietly moved him to another precinct.

“Mario, V is safe and she’s helping us. Earlier when she asked for our help she gave me the key to Vincent’s safe deposit box.”

What tales that will tell.

Chapter 27

Brooklyn

Brooklyn is the fourth largest city in the U.S.

It would be if it was a city. However, it's one of the five boroughs of New York City, with the iconic Brooklyn Bridge connecting it to Manhattan.

Brooklyn Heights, Park Slope, Canarsie, Flatbush and Williamsburg neighborhoods have their own unique lifestyle and residents. From hippies to Orthodox Jewish enclaves, to the Russian community of Brighton Beach, at the end of Ocean Avenue life was complex and diverse.

It was a short drive for Dick, Donnelly and Zero on the FDR Drive onto the Brooklyn Bridge and into those worlds. Populations over the past century had increased significantly thanks to the bridge, the BQE, Brooklyn-Queens Expressway and of course, the subway.

Manhattan had its lights, Empire State Building, United Nations and more as its view. It showcased a window to another world different from their own.

Brooklyn had wonderful parks, museums, and Coney Island with its beaches and boardwalk, and, of course, the World Famous Junior's Cheesecake on Flatbush Avenue.

Many people who lived there never crossed into Manhattan.

Especially many from the mob era. Crime families stayed on their own turf. They were expected to stay and follow orders from the head of the family. When it didn't happen, that's when threats, followed by killings took place.

Detective Donnelly played a tape for Dick and Zero as they headed to Brooklyn. He filled them in about the attempt on V's life and explained that she was tucked away in a safe house.

The tape covered Blanche's last visit to Mario several months earlier. No names were mentioned. She talked of her life in the city, where she lived, and how much longer she would stay there. All code. It only left more questions.

"You sure she doesn't know he's a police informant?"

"Yeah, no way. He's acting as if he'll do whatever she wants."

"Who do you think hired these hit men if the mob's been out of business for years? Someone is apparently still running this family." Dick wondered aloud sitting in the front next to Donnelly, who steered the car hopefully towards some answers.

"First of all, they're not out of business. It's a different business and they've been expanding it secretively for years."

"Dick, do you think Blanche sounds strange?"

"No, but different than when I was with her at Mickey's."

"How?"

"Tough. Like she's giving orders."

"Exactly. No frail old lady for sure."

Zero, meantime, stretched out in the back seat reminded them, "Hey, I want to stop at Junior's for cheesecake. They have my favorite, chocolate mousse."

Dick laughed, "Sure thing, Sweet Cheeks."

"Cute! Hey, we could also stop by a gentlemen's club."

"Sure, Dora would love us doing that."

"Come on, Dick, she won't know." Zero started to flash his holiday bowtie.

"Forget it. We need to see who knows what happened here during the reign of the Cutter Crime Family."

Donnelly drove over the bridge onto Ocean Avenue and would soon be leaving the main highway from Manhattan when he turned off toward Brooklyn Heights.

"Where to first?" Zero asked, clearly wanting it to be Junior's.

"Police headquarters. We have a meeting with a detective I've known for many years and one of his officers. He set it up when I called yesterday. Said they've been aware of an increased undercurrent of activity within a criminal element and been monitoring it."

"What are they involved with?"

"Drugs and diamonds."

“I’d rather have cheesecake.” Zero was determined.

Two hours later the trio headed to a Brooklyn café owned by the same people as the one they frequented on Madison Avenue.

First they met with the Brooklyn detective. “Here are some reports and photographs from the past year regarding Blanche Martin and Gina Torelli. They’ve been involved in meetings with people all the way out to the east end of Long Island. Shaking hands, patting each other on the back. Lots of buddy, buddy stuff.”

“Can you make me a copy of those photos and the report?”

“Already done,” he said and handed Donnelly an envelope. “Anything else we can do to stop these people, count us in.”

Donnelly, Dick and Zero walked into the café, it was quiet being the day before Thanksgiving. There was no sign of Gina Torelli. They had not expected to see her.

They were aware however of a group of men sitting at a round table in the far corner who stared at them when they came in, nodded their heads to each other, and slowly turned away. One quickly made a call on his cell phone.

“I’ll get us coffee to go. I don’t think we should stay here.” Donnelly got up and ordered.

Dick and Zero agreed without saying a word. As they walked out, and got into their car, the man who made the call went to the café window and took photos of them.

"I don't want to start anything yet, not after what we learned earlier. Best we go. We'll catch up with them along with the local police when the time is right."

That would happen soon enough.

Zero was happy. Even though Junior's was mobbed with people picking up Thanksgiving orders for Pumpkin Cheesecake and more, it didn't deter him from his own cheesecake mission.

The gentleman's club was not on the agenda. Although Zero mentioned again it was a good idea.

"Be quiet, Zero, or I'll tell Dora."

The three of them smiled for the first time that day.

Chapter 28

Thanksgiving at the Mansion

The Zimms and Zero, along with Bertie and Carson at Thanksgiving dinner, made a fuss over the sisters who were sitting at the same table. They had managed that with a fifty dollar bill to the day manager.

Dinner started at four P.M. and featured music in the background and cocktails prior to an elaborate catered dinner.

What more could one ask for in their golden years?

Plenty, as it turned out for Dick and Dora and their gang of senior sleuths.

When dessert was served, as pre-arranged, Frankie Socks came in and sat down with them. Bertie had agreed she would leave before dessert so she could innocently keep an eye on the sisters if they left the dining room.

"I'll watch them, Honeybun," Bertie said, glowing and throwing a kiss to Dick.

Socks, dressed in black slacks, gray shirt and black suede jacket, nodded to the sisters. "Hello ladies."

He was shaking. Not that they could notice. He had agreed to this moment in order to push the sisters into wanting to leave.

Donnelly was outside ready to follow anywhere they might go.

They didn't disappoint.

Blanche and Tess looked at each other. The voice was familiar, not the face but there was something about it, startling them. It was enough to make them want to get away from the Mansion immediately. Instincts of many years kicked in again.

"Tess, we need to leave, remember we're expected for dessert elsewhere."

Nodding, she quietly asked Blanche, "Is our ride here?"

"Yes, dear, right out front."

Blanche put her arm through Tess's and headed toward the front entrance with her sister cursing at her.

"Damn it, stop pulling me along. I know how to walk."

"You sure as hell don't know how big a mess everything is since Vincent was murdered."

"Maybe I do."

They were waylaid by Bertie and her walker, pretending to need help.

"Ladies, I left my bag with my key in the dining room. Could you help me go back there?"

"We have no time," shouted an angry Tess.

Her bad temper matched the bad omens facing the family.

They rushed off, practically knocking Bertie over in the process. The extra few minutes gave Dick time to text Donnelly.

"Blanche and Tess are on their way out."

Donnelly, along with two of his officers, had been watching a car parked in front of the Mansion most of the evening.

"They got into a black sedan. We have several unmarked cars set to follow them. We'll be in touch later."

Later he would tell Dick and Dora where the sisters went, what they saw, and how it all played out, like scenes from one of those fabulous 1930s and 1940s noir films.

This was no film.

It was a real life drama with potentially dangerous consequences, especially for the daring senior sleuths who were bound to be in serious peril.

They took too many risks.

Chapter 29

Fuddy Duddy

"Darling, should we follow them?"

"Dora, let the police handle this while we sit here and enjoy our dessert."

"Still…"

"Still, what?"

Dora with her hand on her face, sighed, turned to Zero sitting next to her, and then looked at Socks across from her and Dick now that the sisters had left.

"Still we don't really have any real proof. Perhaps we should take one more look in their condo."

"Oh, for old time's sake?" Dick reached over, hugged her and laughed out loud.

"Exactly. I say the four of us take a stroll. Gentlemen, shall we?"

"No trying to stop her. If we don't go along with her, she'll just go alone."

"Not alone. I always have Zero."

Zero dropped his dessert fork, finished the last of his coffee and stood up, saluting like a good soldier. "Ready at your command, ma'am."

"Aren't we all?" Dick got up with Socks following after the three of them.

They looked like a parade of toy soldiers.

Picking the lock and walking into condo 560, Dick shut the door behind them and stood quiet at first. The sisters were apparently planning on moving. Nothing was in boxes, movers would probably do that, but there was at least a half dozen large black plastic garbage bags filled and tightly tied. Their electricity was off, the phone unplugged, and the room cold and devoid of any life.

"Ya know, my loved ones, I don't think they plan on coming back," Zero commented as Dora and Dick went from room to room opening drawers. Zero and Socks looked under sofa cushions, beds and in kitchen cabinets.

"Nothing?"

"Nah, nothing." Socks and Zero were like a matched set for the moment.

Dick was looking at them, remembering they had always been different in so many ways, the life they each lived. Socks once a hardened criminal, seemingly redeemed and Zero hard working but living life on the edge as a bookie. They were not friends in any way. Their only common interest was Dick and Dora and helping them in their pursuit of criminals and some life saving dramas since they did get into trouble from sleuthing.

Dick's phone buzzed. Shouting to the others, "Let's get out of here now. Their car turned around. They're coming back for some reason."

"But I found something."

"Can you bring it up to our place?"

"Not if they're coming back here."

"Hurry, straighten up any mess we made. Fix those cushions." Dick was yelling orders pulling at Dora to get her out of the condo.

"Oh stop being such a fuddy duddy, darling. We're coming."

"What the hell is a fuddy duddy?" Socks asked and slammed the door shut.

Zero laughed so hard Dick had to push him into the elevator.

Chapter 30

Family Plan

Within twenty minutes, Blanche rushed back to the Mansion and up to her condo while the sedan waited. It took no more than a quick ride to the fifth floor, grabbing a brown leather briefcase sitting on her bed and she was ready to leave again.

Socks in the diner across the street called Dick about her bringing out the briefcase.

That briefcase held papers, a laptop and pictures. It was what Dora had found.

"I didn't have time to look through the papers or photos. You were shouting at us to leave."

"Yes, while you were calling me a fuddy duddy." Dick now laughing and hugging Dora.

Socks stayed at the diner for the rest of the holiday evening. Zero set up the table on the second floor for a poker game.

The only thing near normal about this Thanksgiving was the poker game.

The Martin sisters went to Little Italy first and picked up several people waiting for them in front of what was once a popular restaurant, now closed.

Blanche had opened her car window and shouted at the one woman and two men, "Get into the damn car now, hurry."

Following in an unmarked police car was an officer with Detective Donnelly who told him, "I've got photos of them, sir. The three who just got in and two in the front who picked them up."

A couple of those men were the same as the ones at the Brooklyn café where they had stopped, clearly connecting them to the Martin's and Gina.

"Good. Email the photos to headquarters and to Carson at the paper. Let's see what we can find out about them."

Little Italy, a neighborhood in lower Manhattan was once bustling with dozens of restaurants and shops. Today, the neighborhood consisted of a few gift shops, Italian delis, a couple of restaurants, all surrounded by SOHO, Chinatown and the Lower East Side. The remaining restaurants have a reputation for delicious Italian food in the old-fashioned neighborhood known best to New Yorker's for the San Gennaro Festival each year in September.

The neighborhood had been home to mostly poor Italian immigrants at the turn of the twentieth century. As the mob became financially successful, the bosses moved to Brooklyn and Queens. Years later others would head east out to Long Island.

Mob bosses and the higher ups in their organizations found it easy to live in these new neighborhoods. They could hide in plain sight in beautiful brick homes, some gated with alarms and security guards. Other less pretentious homes, housed people equally dangerous.

Donnelly began filling his officer in about some of the characters involved in this drama, explaining why they were in pursuit of them.

"It's complicated by layers of secrecy and deceit. Blanche had been married to the head of one of the most dangerous mobs and most deadly of men, Cutter. It had been rumored by many he had killed his first wife and mother of his children. Her body was never found and certainly no one in the family dared talk about it."

"Did anyone ever report her missing?"

"Never. Probably didn't want to risk disappearing too."

"Cutter must have been very young when he began his infamous career."

"Got his nickname when he was only fourteen and took a knife to another fourteen year old. It was a girl who refused to go out with him. Told him he was creepy."

"Did she die?"

"No, but she and her family moved away as soon as she was out of the hospital."

"Did she tell anyone he attacked her?"

"No one snitched on him. Already almost six feet tall he scared the hell out of the other kids and it left him feeling powerful. At sixteen he got a tattoo of a knife on his neck and soon organized a gang of boys who terrorized the neighborhood shops and schools."

"Was he ever arrested back then?"

"Sure. No matter how often the police showed up, he proclaimed his innocence. And so did everyone else. They always had an alibi for him. Fear ruled his neighborhood and by the time he was twenty the fear extended beyond."

"What about other mobs at that point?"

"By age twenty-two Cutter's mob took control of the area's prostitution, and drug trafficking and arranged for any murders needed to keep everyone in line. Then as mob wars began he became more driven, more crazed. Killing was easy for him. It was also easy for some of the other mobsters."

"What ended it?"

"Too many people murdered. Finally a big police sweep of the mobs. There were a couple confidential informants, plus a strong witness for the prosecution. Cutter swore revenge, declaring it in horrifyingly explicit language."

"Did anyone take over for him after he went to prison?"

"We always thought so, but they went deep underground for many years and we could never find a way in until recently. Okay, best we concentrate on following them. They're headed to Brooklyn."

"Still don't you think it's strange, all this activity suddenly?"

Detective Donnelly, nodded his head in agreement, as he watched the sedan with the sisters and others turn left into a long driveway, leading to a large red brick house, with a gate and guards including a couple huge watchdogs.

As they drove by, the officer took more photos and forwarded them.

"Sir, now what?"

"Back to the city. See that truck up ahead? It's one of ours taping the conversations in the house. We have what we need for now. Get me information about the photos as soon as possible."

Family values of a different sort were a major topic inside the secure red brick house in Brooklyn.

Problems Tess caused and blamed Blanche. It was hard sometimes for those listening in to identify who was talking.

"The present situation with Drugs for Diamonds needs to be handled. We need to stop any further investigation of the family. Remember we have over a half dozen shell companies they don't know anything about and I want to keep it that way."

"What are you suggesting?"

"Get rid of Dick and Dora Zimmerman. Your people so far have failed. Correct that."

"What about that intrusive idiot Zero with the silly blinking bow tie?"

"Get rid of him too."

"Our family has survived all these years because we trusted each other, kept our secrets, did as demanded, remained apart from society, and built a financial empire in the process. I want the problems terminated immediately."

The head of the family was damn angry.

"Next time we meet, I want to finalize our expansion plans."

"And the police?"

"Make it look as if it's their fault those people have been killed. I'll get a story planted in Manhattan media making the police seem weak and incompetent."

"How're you going to do that?"

"I have my sources. You take care of the killings."

Those in the sedan knew they had been followed but kept quiet for fear of more anger and outrage at the meeting. After all, the car couldn't follow them into the private driveway.

They had paid no attention to the electric company truck parked down the road.

"Get to the city and do what I told you. Kill them! If you fail you'll be next."

They believed him. He was hard and mean. They knew from experience he was unforgiving of any mistakes.

His was one of the voices hard for the police to identify.

Chapter 31

Conversation with Dora

"Dick said he didn't think you would mind if I visited with you," said Dora.

"Come in."

"It's a poker night."

"I know."

"Do you know a lot of detectives?"

"Met a few over the years."

"Dick thinks I go overboard in what he calls sleuthing. I find it difficult to let go of solving a problem."

"Or a crime."

"Yes, I'm afraid so," she said, laughing. Dora was fascinated by the person and the room she was sitting in as they talked.

"Did you like your work?"

"Very much so. When it was over it was over. Times change. I'm fortunate to have had the experience."

"Still, you seem connected to all you did. The photos in here are wonderful and amazing reminders."

Dora walked around the room. On one wall were dozens of photos, many of people she recognized.

"They are. Makes me happy to have them, to have had time with them."

"Did you learn a lot about the industry when you were involved?"

"Sure. The work is not all that complicated. It's probably similar to what you realized as a judge. People allow their ambitions or greed to make situations difficult and then they become complicated."

"They do, don't they? That and an almost righteous sense of self can motivate the worse behaviors."

"Let me ask you a question."

"Okay." Dora was curious about him, why shouldn't he be curious about her.

"Why do you like what you do? Even though you're retired as a judge you continue in similar pursuits."

"Justice. The desire for fairness which is not always easy to accomplish."

"You know you're a dichotomy of traits from what I can see."

"Such as? You don't think I'm going to leave here without your insight on that?"

He laughed and quite heartily.

"You're stubborn and confident. You have a heart full of love and probably gratitude while you're also extremely impatient."

"Is that such a bad thing?"

"Only when you allow it to lead you into trouble, which I suspect it has a number of times."

"True."

"Nevertheless, you know, you're not always as careful as you should be."

"Also true."

"I suspect it won't stop you in the future."

This time Dora laughed as she got up to leave, thanking him for his time. She didn't want to stay too long. He was no longer a young man.

Dora smiled and leaned over to kiss him goodbye on the cheek, leaving a huge smile on his face.

Leaving didn't stop her from thinking about their conversation. Yes she did have a flair for getting into troublesome situations.

Well, she and Dick both did.

As Dick would soon find out once again.

Chapter 32

The Sleuths Plan

Friday morning after Thanksgiving a group of them were in the Zimms apartment.

"I would think you would all be exhausted from playing poker half the night."

Dora told them about her questioning other people who lived in the Mansion about Blanche and Tess.

"All I got was some liked them others thought they were mean or secretive and didn't like them at all."

"We need to find out what they're really up to." Zero and Carson stretched out on the sofa and nodded yes. Both were too tired to do much more. Donnelly chatted on his cell phone, checking on V.

Zero was humming "My Way." Dick turned and gave him a dirty look. Dora already thought Dick would do something dangerous without her. Then again Dick thought the same thing about Dora.

Dora stopped pacing, glared at Dick and Zero and clearly agitated began, "Listen, all of you, especially you two jokers. They're on to us. We know that from their trying to kidnap me. We need to outsmart them and not keep bumbling about hoping they turn into two lovely old ladies who mean no harm. Because I believe they do."

"I'm all for that, sweetheart. We need to surprise them. I don't think these are two lovely old ladies at all. They're trouble and they've created quite a mess for themselves giving us a chance to make it even bigger."

"I have an idea."

"What would that be, Officer?" Dick did his best imitation of charming.

Ignoring him, Donnelly said, "We'll need help, but as the only police official in this room, I do expect, desire more like, your participation."

Donnelly, serious and determined, took over the impromptu meeting. Zero and Carson quieted. Dick got up to get some coffee.

"I want to have the inside of the meatpacking plant dug up tomorrow. I got a search warrant for it yesterday."

"Your reason, Mr. Detective?"

"Keep it up, Dick, and I'll lock you up for assaulting an officer of the law."

Dick did keep quiet, at least for the moment.

"I'm sure there are more bodies in that old plant. Bodies that could lead to evidence against the Group."

"*The Group*? What group? Who are they? What are you talking about?" Zero blurted out.

"The Drugs for Diamonds crime family, I believe, is behind these recent murders."

"Oh, them."

"Yes, them. It includes the Martin Sisters, Gina Torelli and whoever else was with them at that meeting in Brooklyn. We have the photos of some of them, the house where they met, plus their car model and license plate. I had an electric company truck park down the road. It was set up for surveillance and we heard them discussing plans for expanding their Drugs for Diamonds operation."

"Clever, Chief. When did you arrange that?" Again it was Zero with the question.

"Hey, I'm not just another pretty face."

Donnelly was talking with his hands waving in the air. He was a man with a mission to eliminate the crime family who was killing people and threatening the safety of his friends.

"We set the operation up a couple days ago so it would be ready, had them on standby. As soon as we started following them, my officer texted the team in the truck to follow, staying far enough behind not to create any suspicion. We had prearranged for the team to be parked a couple blocks from where our suspects would be meeting."

Donnelly raised his eyebrows at Zero and the others and told them what the police overheard from a group of criminals, liars, and murderers who secretly led the crime family group identified as Drugs for Diamonds based in Brooklyn and Little Italy.

Donnelly walked over to where he has set up his laptop computer on the Zimms' coffee table, opened it and clicked a button.

"We finally have proof of some of their illegal activities. We're still not sure who the top person is though. They carefully protect this mysterious figure."

"What's next?" Dora pulled over one of the chairs and sat in front of the computer in order to look closely at each scene as it played out.

Donnelly paused the computer. "We don't want to overplay our hand until we're sure who the ringleader is. Most of the people are in the background. We can't identify their voices. A few we can, plus they mention names."

Clicking the laptop again, the recording continued. "It's the damn photos you saved of Cutter and those kids." Gina was screaming at Blanche. "Then tango lessons. Really, Blanche? What the hell were you thinking anyhow? Some young guy is whirling you around on the dance floor, bending you over like a freaking pretzel and you decide to fall for his scam? What an idiot."

A couple of male voices could be heard in the background, mumbling something the recording wasn't able to pick up clearly. They sounded determined and nasty. That much was obvious from the tone of their voices.

"Shut up, Gina. You're a fool. I didn't save those photos."

"Then who did? Cause I sure didn't."

"Tess did, and I only recently realized it. Same with the tango lessons. Yes, I was having fun, but never was I taking Alphonse seriously. I knew he was a con man."

"Okay, how did this mess happen?" Gina's high pitched voice grew higher, angrier.

"Tess, for her own reasons. She kept those old photos. I never realized it. I didn't explore her closets or drawers. Then, I found out she sent a note to Alphonse as if it came from me, professing my deep fondness for him. It said I was excited about going into business with him and invited him to stay with us if he ever wanted."

"I'm not sure what you're getting at, Blanche. He *was* at your apartment. That's where he was found murdered."

"Believing I had invited him, he came up with a lie about having to be out of his apartment. Tess made all this fuss about it like she was shocked and angry he wanted to spend time at our place."

"How do you know?"

"She admitted it to me after he was dead. Laughing and telling me she would let all of you know I had been played for a fool. Tess handed me the note she sent him with some X's on it for kisses. I saved it. Here, you can see. It's in her handwriting. She thought I threw it out in disgust."

"What about V and Vincent?"

"She also made arrangements with them, pretending I gave the order to murder them. Of course when the damn alarm went off it caused havoc at the Mansion and created a problem for us. Mostly for me at the time, which is what Tess ultimately intended. She knew I had pushed for Vincent to get a job there. I gave him an excellent recommendation. This way he could help with the business."

Tess suddenly grew hysterical knowing she had been caught. Caught indeed.

"It was that damn Dick Zimmerman thinking he was saving us when we got off the elevator," she yelled. "We pretended to be crying and upset. He took us to that bar as if we were a couple of weak, miserable old ladies. He's a fool. His wife and their buddy Zero are real pains, both asking lots of questions about us. They found Alphonse murdered in our condo before we could get rid of him.

"Blanche should be replaced. She's losing it. Dancing around like a slut with this hot young man," Tess continued yelling, now jamming her finger at her sister.

"It's all her fault. She always thought she was better than me. I'm the one Cutter should have married, not her."

Blanche went over and smacked Tess so hard she fell to the floor. "You stupid woman, you really think you can take over here? You're ridiculous and disgusting. Get her out of here."

A couple of men could be heard dragging a ranting Tess out of the room. There was no way to see where they took her or what they did, but the shuffling and banging sounds were clear. Then silence for almost five minutes.

Gina, finally far more restrained, restarted the meeting and the discussion regarding plans to move the Drugs for Diamond business elsewhere.

"We've already checked out several places. We'll have more information as requested by next meeting."

Several people tossed out their preference for the new location.

"I like Miami."

"Vegas would be better, more easy money there."

"San Francisco or Los Angeles offer benefits too. Big cities with diverse populations."

After two more hours, the meeting ended with an agreement to meet in Little Italy early the next week.

"I don't want to postpone this anymore, understand?" the unknown man demanded in the background.

Watching and listening to this meeting left everyone uneasy. They were pretty sure of Tess's fate.

Shadows once again appeared to leap onto the walls in the Zimms' apartment, from the combination of the lights inside and the sky darkening from clouds of snow falling outside. It felt like a black and white noir film being made.

"Shawn, I assume you'll soon have more information from the medical examiner," Dick asked, ever the prosecutor.

"I expect something from forensics regarding the DNA and fingerprints where Vincent was found in the garage," Donnelly replied.

"By the way, has the hit man you arrested for trying to kill V told you anything?"

"Nothing. He immediately asked for an attorney. We have him dead to rights. No pun intended, in attempting to kill her. His attorney will try to get him out on bail but we have proof he's a flight risk and a serious threat to the public."

"Shawn, how about if we ask Carson for another favor?" Dora, growing animated, knew she had a really good idea.

"You guys are killing me," Carson said. "What do you want now?"

"Can you get a photographer from your paper to take photos of the meatpacking plant search? If the police find bodies buried in there as they suspect, they could be from the past thirty years. Could be a great photo-op and story."

"Great idea," replied both Dick and Donnelly. Even Carson agreed.

It could turn out to be a front-page story in Carson's paper with a full spread of photos inside along with additional stories about crime families in New York over the past hundred years. It could also be intended to provoke the present crime family.

The local and national television news media could also pick up the story showing a team of police and coroners carrying bodies out of the plant. It would be a gruesome sight and the television reporters in particular could play it up big time.

"We are about to show some photos you may find objectionable."

It would provoke the Group into frantic and reckless actions.

The question was, who would those actions hurt the most?

The Group, or those seeking and equally determined to shut them down permanently?

Dora joked to Dick, “See, darling, we’re only the bait.”

Chapter 33

Hit

Unlocking the door to his condo Dick heard it. The sound a gun makes moments before someone is about to shoot it.

"I dropped to the floor, although they managed to hit me in the arm. Fortunately I was able to quickly push the door to our condo open and slide in like a damn puppy rubbing its bottom. Then I slammed the door shut," said Dick, clearly annoyed.

He called Zero. "I've been shot and personally I'm pissed. A perfectly nice jacket ruined. Get Donnelly. Don't leave Dora alone. Get up here. I'm waiting for the police."

The three of them, the Zimms and Zero, had been out having lunch at their favorite sushi restaurant on the Upper West Side. They had all agreed they needed a break from the Mansion and turkey in any form.

"Dick, I'm going shopping, see you later."

"Lady D, I'll join you." Zero wanted to talk to her about the synagogue event on Sunday evening he thought was to honor Dick.

It was fine with Dick. He was ready for a nap, hoping he wouldn't get cornered by Bertie, hugging and making what he called *goo-goo* eyes at him.

Instead of a nap, he was waiting for Detective Donnelly who arrived sirens and guns blazing. He found Dick in his condo nursing his minor wound and his ego with a drink and a grudge.

"I need a description of the man you saw shoot at you."

"Dark clothes, dark hair under a Mets baseball cap, sunglasses, about 5'10." It could have easily been a woman or a man. Whoever it is owes me a new jacket!"

"I'm sure they feel so guilty about it they're out shopping for you right now."

"Sarcasm to a man who's been badly wounded?"

"Only thing wounded at the moment is your ego and your precious jacket. I've got two police officers stationed downstairs, and one at your door until we figure out what's going on here."

"What's going on, dear man, is someone tried to kill me."

"You did suggest you were bait."

"Not funny. Probably thinks we're too involved in helping solve these murders. Or maybe they don't like the way I look. Damn if I know."

"All of you need to be extra careful," warned Donnelly, looking at Dora who had rushed in with Zero and was fussing over Dick.

"I know you're a tough guy, sweetheart, but this should be looked at by a doctor."

"I'm fine. Just annoyed."

One thing was certain after Donnelly told him about following the Martin sisters to Little Italy then to Brooklyn: Their secrets were sinister, their connections dangerous, their actions threatening.

Chapter 34

The Will and Message

"Give the envelope to the police in case the family tries to hurt you."

Inside Vincent's safe deposit box along with his will and a huge amount of cash, all left for V, was a large manila envelope marked *POLICE*. Inside were unbelievable details on the Cutter crime family.

Details as far back as the time when Cutter had been convicted. There were names and addresses of top people involved in the buying and selling of Drugs for Diamonds, lists of people murdered by them and the location of millions of dollars hidden off shore from the Cayman Islands to Switzerland.

It was late Friday evening with dinner ordered in from Mickey's. Donnelly wanted to show Dick and Dora what he found and heard before he was called about Dick's shooting.

"He must have known a time would come when he and V could have a problem with the family." Dick was curious if there was any physical evidence they could use.

Donnelly let him look through the several dozen pages of documents Vincent left. “Unfortunately, more physical evidence is needed to arrest and convict these people. Surprisingly he didn’t name the head of the family. Makes me very curious about why?”

“What about Mario?”

Mario’s voice was on the tape he made for Detective Donnelly after hearing Vincent had been murdered. Clearly shaken, in a whispered voice he told them, “Vincent and Valentina are my younger brother and sister. The family decided on different last names for obvious reasons.”

Donnelly was playing the tape for Dick and Dora. Zero was napping on the sofa.

“Remember, Cutter’s birth name was Christian Russo. He later changed his last name to Martin in an effort to confuse the police and press.”

“What about Vincent and Valentina?”

“Blair was Cutter’s first wife’s maiden name. She was killed not long after V was born. We all have the same mother and father, but different last names because they thought it would be harder to connect us.”

“Is V okay? Is she safe? Were you able to help her?”

“Wait until you hear this.” Donnelly wanted to be sure he had Dick’s attention.

Zero responded with a loud snore.

"One more thing about the old meatpacking plant, it's owned under the name of Blair. I think you'll be shocked with what you find."

It was more than shocking, it was gruesome.

Power struggles within this crime family, same as any other, were nothing new, only lately this one was gaining momentum, almost getting out of hand. Recent actions had caused an unexpected frenzy of activity by the family and by the police. Then there were others involved in helping the police to investigate the murders of Alphonse and Vincent, meaning the Zimms.

Over the years their power struggles included setting others up for crimes and murders they hadn't committed.

According to information Vincent left, Mario Russo had been framed. Set up to take the fall involving a big drug bust. It was a crime he didn't commit.

Donnelly put in another call to Mario and played the conversation for him.

"Drugs were found in my home and car. I was found guilty as you know, and here I am." Mario told his story to Donnelly as Dick and Dora listened.

"I'm not sure who set me up, but I have a pretty good idea it was Tess Martin, Blanche's sister. I couldn't prove it. All the evidence was against me at the time."

"Did you ask anyone in the family for help?"

"Vincent. He said he would check around for me."

"Did he find out anything?"

"He was told to stay out of it, or he and V would also be in trouble."

"But why would Tess want to do this to you?"

"To hurt Blanche. She was always jealous of her but she was great at pretending she cared about her. I saw lots of that behavior when I was a kid. If I tried to say anything she would smack me or threaten she would see V was sent away. Where, I had no idea, so I kept quiet."

Mario and Donnelly agreed it was time for him to make a call, and yes it could be taped.

"I know plenty of secrets about the family that I overheard over the years as I was growing up." Mario was furious and rightfully so.

"Gina, I think the person causing you some of your recent problems is also responsible for framing me. Vincent and I talked before he was killed."

"Did he tell you what was happening with Tess and Blanche?"

"Yes."

Gina was tough with a mean temper and that wasn't going to be good for some people. "Things are going to change, Mario. I promise you. I want you back here with us."

"I'd sure like that. Just get me out of here."

He wanted as much ammunition against the family who'd framed him as possible. He had no intention of being part of the family again, not ever. It was going to be up to Detective Donnelly to help him and V get away from them.

At the Mansion, Bertie was desperately calling Carson. She had been sleuthing since early Saturday morning as Dick had suggested. Since she adored him, of course, she did as he asked, always throwing him a kiss or two with a twinkle in her eye.

"Bertie, I need you to keep watch to see if anything is happening regarding the Martin sisters."

Moving close to other resident's conversations, walking around the Mansion, and watching and listening, it had suddenly and unexpectedly paid off.

"Carson, get over here. Call Dick. Hurry. It's urgent."

Answering on the third ring and sounding annoyed, he said, "What now, Grandma?"

Bertie didn't take nonsense from anyone including her grandson.

"Damn it, Carson, don't treat me like I'm stupid because I'm old. A moving truck has pulled into the back of the Mansion and is loading everything from Blanche and Tess's condo. Neither of them is here. They never came back after they left Thanksgiving dinner."

"Grandma, stand in their way. Stop them somehow. I'll call Dick and the police right away. There could be evidence about the murders in that stuff."

Bertie had been eavesdropping on the movers.

"Where are we taking all this stuff?"

"We were told to take it to some church and the black garbage bags are to go to the city dump."

"Well if they don't want any of it, once it's on the truck let's take what we want."

"Hey you guys, any stuff I can have?" Bertie interjected.

"Lady, get out of our way. We need to finish and move on with this junk."

"If it's junk, why can't I have some?"

"Because it doesn't belong to us."

"Can I look in these bags? I could use some new clothes. Maybe they're throwing some away." Bertie was doing her best to slow them down.

"No, you can't look in any of the bags. Mow get away."

Bertie was leaning on her walker, pretending it was hard for her to move very fast.

"I swear, lady, I'll pick you up and move you myself."

Bertie pretended not to hear. At almost ninety she could get away with a lot, she once told Carson.

"No one's going to move her anywhere. Get off the truck. I'm Detective Donnelly and I have a search warrant on the way for everything from the condo."

It had taken him less than fifteen minutes to get there; one of his officers would have the warrant there within the hour.

"What are we supposed to do? We've been hired to move everything from that condo and we were told we'd get a bonus if we got it done quickly."

Donnelly shrugged his shoulders as the disgruntled and annoyed men stepped away so the truck and everything on it from the Martin sisters' condo was searched.

"Sir, look at this."

One of the officers searching the garbage bags handed it to him. "It's the black and gold knife you told us to look for in this stuff. The knife's handle is inlaid with different colored gemstones shaped like a large hook."

Donnelly thanked him, and had him put it in an evidence bag,

The blade was known as a needlepoint blade, or dagger. It had two very sharp edges and was easily used for stabbing. Some people used them in wartime, for close combat and self-defense. Then again this knife had also been used in war. Mob wars.

"It's an exact duplicate of the knife we found protruding from Alphonse's chest."

Evidence against the sisters was mounting up.

Still the head of the family was a mystery.

Dick gave Bertie a big bear hug while Donnelly watched the bags being searched. The entire truck would be confiscated by the police. Forensics was already on notice it was coming.

The movers were none too thrilled.

No one cared about that.

"Bertie, you are our angel. Great sleuthing, young lady."

She was beaming.

"I'll take another one of those hugs, darling." That from her secret love, as she referred to Dick.

Bertie with rouged cheeks, deep pink lipstick, dressed in a pink sweat suit to match was moved and beaming when her grandson hugged her and told her, "I'm so proud of you. We all are."

"You can't take any of this stuff," the grumbling movers were told again. "It's evidence from a crime scene, a murder took place in that condo."

Armed with the search warrant, the truck was transported to the police garage in Midtown. Later they would find more evidence of Tess's craziness.

"Dick, you won't believe what we found in one of the dresser drawers under some clothes," Donnelly said. "Tess had a diary and it reads like dialogue from a movie script."

"Can I see it?"

"Sure, get over here. Bring Dora. This is really something."

The three of them read page after page. There was only one or two lines at the most for any given date. The statements getting odder and odder.

"I think she's truly crazy. Look at what she wrote, years ago till now."

"He should be mine"

"Should have married me."

"That's why I killed her."

"Blanche is jealous of me."

"I'll kill them both someday."

"Glad he went to prison."

"Hope someone murders him in there."

"I pretend to feel bad."

"Found a way to hurt her really bad."

"Set Mario up."

"Save photos."

"Kill Alphonse."

"Use one of those knives."

"Blame Vincent."

"Destroy V."

"Ruin Blanche."

"Tell the family she's crazy."

"I can't read anymore of this garbage. Who writes stuff like this? Where is Tess Martin? Aren't you bringing her in for questioning," Dora asked, disgusted.

"The police can't find her anywhere."

They would soon enough.

Chapter 35

Sins of the Past in The Meatpacking Plant

Cutter had left behind his wife, children, legal advisors, a few low level associates and a threat of revenge promised to those who had betrayed him.

Carson called Donnelly, then Dick and of course that meant Dora too. "Meet me in an hour at the police station. I found a treasure trove of information on Blanche and Tess, their life and relationships with the mob, and how Cutter met Blanche, while he was still married to his first wife. There's numerous newspaper articles with photos in the archives from when Cutter had been arrested and put on trial. Many photos showing him ranting and threatening the police and everyone else he felt deserved it. Blanche is in the background."

Sitting in one of the small station conference rooms, the only windows up high and another small table with plastic glasses and water pitcher, the four of them sat and looked at what Carson wanted to show them.

"Recent years show Blanche at various fundraising events for some prominent politicians, their arms around her, or hugging her. Tess is never in any of those photos.

Blanche is described as a philanthropist, a generous lady who cared dearly about her city and its people."

"She sure fooled a lot of people. She's been hanging out with some heavy hitters in the political and business world for many years."

"We've figured out they stayed at the Mansion as a pretense to appear like two elderly, even a bit ditzy sisters. When they discovered you and Dora had moved in, Blanche and Gina decided they were going to have the two of you killed. They remembered Dick had been the prosecutor against Cutter and instrumental in getting Frankie Socks to testify." Donnelly was helping Carson spread the photos out on the rectangular table as Dora kept looking again and again at a couple of them that seemed to bother her.

"Blanche had a long and vengeful memory," Donnelly told them. "While the family was being watched recently, she too had been doing some watching of her own. That was how it happened that two men followed Dick and Dora to Chinatown, then attempted to grab Dora off the elevator and of course tried to kill Dick as he went into his condo."

"Apparently they knew we were helping investigate Alphonse's murder," Dora said, raising her head and looking right at Donnelly.

"Sure. They also knew about our visits to Sing Sing and out to Brooklyn. Fortunately not about Mario being an informant or the surveillance truck. Thank goodness for that."

"Do you think some of her political and business buddies are involved in Drugs for Diamonds?"

"I certainly do. We believe it goes pretty high up the food chain."

"Planning on some arrests soon?"

"Absolutely. We want this tied up tight so we're keeping surveillance on a handful of people and locations until we have everything we need to take them down for good."

Frankie Socks was thankful too. Dressed in jeans, a Mets baseball jacket and cap, he was standing nearby, out of sight, watching a whole lot of police close off the block surrounding the old meatpacking plant. They were dressed in evidence suits and carrying shovels in preparation for hauling out whatever they might find.

Socks had stayed away from the Mansion since Thanksgiving. It was Dick who called him about the police going to search the meatpacking plant.

"Watch if you want, I figured it would interest you, but stay out of sight. There's sure to be plenty of media and photographers around. It promises to be a big news story."

What they would find seemed unreal to everyone involved in the search.

As they opened the doors to the plant, the smell was almost overwhelming. Two of the officers went around opening every window, leaving the front and back doors open as well and shouted, "It smells like death in here. Get some Vick's for all of us."

Socks watched it all.

So did Dick and Dora with Zero. Dick saw Socks down the street and nodded to him. They too stayed outside the perimeter of the crime scene tape. They saw Carson go in with his paper's photographer and when they came out they looked genuinely horrified at what they had seen.

Dora put her arm through Dick's and moved closer to him, both of them wearing heavy winter coats and knit hats. The chill was from more than the cold November air and a freezing, drizzling rain. Death became a dark cloud over them.

The photos in the newspaper showed the meatpacking plant, unused for many years, dilapidated, with crumbling walls and caved in ceilings. Old, empty boxes were scattered everywhere.

Inside an unlocked back room of the plant it was even darker, more ominous, with walls crumbling. Eventually large plastic bags with dead bodies inside were discovered buried beneath hidden floorboards in a far corner.

Carson Gladstone's headline: *Dozens of Mob Hits Discovered.*

The front-page story began "Dozens of buried bodies were found in an abandoned meatpacking plant, some appearing to be from as long as thirty years ago. There are victims everywhere and it will take weeks to identify all of the bodies. Authorities are working to prepare indictments against an organized crime family that has been active for thirty years."

A quote from Detective Donnelly would only say "We received an anonymous and reliable tip."

Another reporter who called Donnelly asked, "Who gave you the tip?"

Donnelly shouted angrily, "What don't you understand about anonymous?"

"Dick, the evidence we have is being carefully sorted through and will be catalogued by our forensic team, headed by Dr. Blythe Morrison."

Donnelly later told Dick, "We believe Cutter's first wife was one of the oldest bodies discovered. One of the newest dead bodies buried there is Tess Martin."

Donnelly did answer one reporter's question. "Who owns this plant, Detective?"

"Blanche Martin."

"Is she aware of what's buried in there?"

"We haven't been able to interview her yet. Her attorney said she is in a state of shock and cannot comment at this time."

Blanche and her attorney were in a state of panic was more like it.

The as yet unknown head of this crime family was beyond furious.

He was demanding answers.

"How the hell did you let this happen? Someone is going to pay for this."

Chapter 36

Dora and Blythe

"Blythe, can you meet for coffee in the morning? Don't let Donnelly know I've called."

"Dora, meet me at the City Diner two blocks from my building, nine A.M."

Blythe hung up. The work in front of her was more than a challenge. It would take her team of coroners and forensic experts days to autopsy and identify the more than forty bodies found in the meatpacking plant. Some might never be identified.

Something was bothering Dora. Something about the photos she had seen of Blanche cozying up with different political figures, one in particular. A big name politician seemed to have his arm around her in an odd way. Donnelly gave her copies of two photos she asked for figuring there was no harm in her having them.

Did he really forget this was Dora Zimmerman?

She always had a reason capable of getting her and others in trouble especially when it came to a murder investigation.

"I need your unbiased opinion. All my years as a judge I learned to look at people's faces and body language."

Dora placed two photos on the table in front of Blythe. Sitting in a booth across from each other, each with coffee only.

"I know you're crazy busy. Only before I bring anyone else's attention to them, I wanted you to look at the man in these photos. I believe he could be the top guy in the crime family being investigated, and directly or indirectly, responsible for many of those bodies in your morgue."

Blythe sat quietly staring at the photos, same as when a body first came into the morgue. She once told Dora, "They can usually tell me a story of how they lived and how they died. If they've been murdered, it's up to others to figure out who's responsible for that."

"Please feel free to tell me if I've gone off the deep end."

"Dora, he's been a political fixture in the city and state for years. I'm sure you've been in his company a number of times, as have I. Our work has brought us in contact with many leading politicians over the years."

"I know. He's a political powerhouse."

"You would need a lot more than these photos to prove he's involved in any criminal activity."

"In this one, it's like he has a hold on her, not in a friendly way."

Scrutinizing the photos, thanks to her years as a coroner, she too could read faces and body language, even if from a far different perspective than Dora's. Dora was counting on Blythe's experience and perception as a professional.

"I haven't mentioned it to Dick. He'll either go all out nuts on me for considering it, or else believe me and go after him like a dog with a bone. You know how he is when it comes to crime and punishment. And protecting me."

"He won't let go until everything is solved and wrapped in a neat package. Bad guys arrested. Bad guys go to prison."

"Blythe, be honest, what's your thought on the people in these photos?"

"Find proof. Real proof. You need hard evidence the police can take to the D.A. My agreeing with you, which I admit I do, certainly isn't enough. By the way, if you check out her other hand, she's squeezing it tight as if she wishes she could punch him. At the very least helping her keep some control over the moment."

"Exactly."

"What are you going to do?"

"I have an idea."

"Not sure I like the sharp tone of your voice. Knowing you it's probably risky. Dick would kill both of us if anything happened to you."

Dr. Blythe Morrison got up and went over to hug Dora.

"Have to get back to that mess of bodies. Please be careful. Love."

"I will. Same to you."

Dora was to meet Zero at eleven to pick up his tuxedo. She would ask for his help.

Like he would say no to her.

Chapter 37

A Dangerous Plan

So far Zero was clueless that he was to be honored by the rabbi and the synagogue for his many years of generous donations to them, believing it was an event to honor Dick.

Dora confirmed the details with the rabbi, including the home where the event was to occur that had been overtaken by caterers and florists. At least two hundred people were expected to attend the posh evening.

"You have to wear the tuxedo. Stop fidgeting." Dora and Zero were at the tuxedo rental shop on Madison Avenue in Midtown Manhattan.

"I look ridiculous."

"You look charming and handsome. You'll make Dick very proud. If you don't stop complaining, I'm going to invite Bertie to be your date."

Laughing and pushing him into the dressing room to change, she finalized the rental arrangements.

"I want a purple cummerbund," he demanded, pouting and sounding like a three year old.

"Fine, you can have a purple one if you stop being fussy."

"Why isn't Dick here?"

"Because he owns a tuxedo."

Walking out of the shop, Dora turned to Zero. "I need to ask you to go somewhere with me tomorrow."

Slipping her arm into his, walking on Manhattan's somewhat icy streets, cold air swirling about them, she was telling him her idea and why.

"Dora, my dear, if we get caught we'll be chopped meat, no questions asked."

"Then darling, we better not get caught."

She knew he wouldn't, couldn't say no to her, even though it was more than a daring plan. It was dangerous. She had shown him the photos, and told him what she thought about the man in them.

One thing Zero was certain of, even if she got angry with him, he was going to let Dick know where they were going and what they were planning on doing.

Dr. Blythe Morrison had also decided if she didn't hear from Dora by early Monday afternoon, she too would call Dick to check on her. More like tattle on her she thought.

For now she had bodies that needed her attention.

"Okay, Zero. My plan. Monday afternoon we'll sit in one of the Italian bakeries, have coffee, and go in a few shops as if we're looking for gifts."

"Then what do you propose we do? We can't show those photos around."

"We'll just mention his name and comment what a good man he is, ask if he ever comes around here."

"Come on, Dora. You think no one is going to get suspicious?"

"We'll be outside, in daylight. What could possibly happen?"

"Famous last words, darling."

Dora wrapped her warm cashmere scarf tighter around her neck, a colder wind was coming in off the East River.

Zero the bookie, shook his head, raised his eyebrows and didn't say another word as they hailed a cab back to the Mansion.

This was one situation he had no intention of betting on. He didn't like the odds of what could happen.

Socks saw a man and a woman watching the Mansion from inside the diner. He was in a booth; they were sitting on stools whispering, looking out the window decorated with a huge snowman. He could tell they were carrying guns from the bulges in their jacket pockets.

"Detective Donnelly, Dick said to call you if I saw anything that might need your attention."

An hour later Donnelly and three police officers arrived and quietly and quickly took the two would be assassins out of the diner and arrested them for carrying weapons without a permit. The hit was intended to be a loud statement. "Don't mess with us, we're ready for you."

They had been ordered to take out Dick and Dora Zimmerman.

Donnelly would tell Dick about it later that evening.

Mario later identified them as members of the family. They were around his age, started out as kids same as he did, with parents who set their lives in motion.

It was Socks that surprised the appreciative detective.

"How did you know they were carrying?"

"Not my first rodeo. I grew up around guys like that. They were brazen about carrying guns. Thought it made them big men."

Chapter 38

For Justice

As they got into the Town Car to go to the event, Zero was fussing. “I don’t know why I need to wear this ridiculous penguin suit since Dick is the one being honored.”

He was shocked when he walked in to the beautiful Upper East Side apartment filled with people who belonged to the synagogue. There were also friends from the Mansion, his daughter and close to a dozen politicians who courted the Jewish vote each election. When the rabbi came up to greet Zero, he realized he had been had.

He turned to look at Dick and Dora, who were grinning from ear to ear, standing by the entrance to the apartment.

“No way you can escape.”

With tears in his eyes, wearing his tuxedo and purple cummerbund, Zero for a change was speechless. Many gave brief talks of appreciation and there were acknowledgment plaques from the mayor and two state senators.

The most moving part of the evening was when three people, who had been recipients of money he donated, each spoke passionately about how it had changed and improved their lives.

"His generosity and good heartedness has been a remarkable gift to the synagogue and to my husband and me. Our friendship has been endearing and enduring."

Dora, dressed in a stunning, black silk cocktail dress, her only jewelry, ironically, a pair of dangling diamond earrings, was definitely in tears.

In presenting him with the humanitarian award, the rabbi spoke of a world that needed more justice, and men and women like Zero who aided its cause.

"The Torah says, 'Do unto others as you would have them do unto you.' All the rest is commentary."

"I'm honored, thank you. Speaking of justice, I promise to get even with the Zimmerman's for tricking me about this evening." Zero knew how to lighten the mood.

"Dick, I'm so proud of our Zero. At least for one evening, some balance has been brought into our lives. The insanity of the murders and threatens from the crime family has been set aside to celebrate a dear friend's unselfish good deeds."

Dora had her arm through Dick's and he turned to kiss her.

It was an important night in this Jewish home where they were celebrating one person's acts of kindness and generosity.

The man Dora believed was head of the crime family was smiling and shaking hands, having his photo taken with Zero and the rabbi.

Dora flinched when she saw him.

He didn't miss that.

Outside watching were those who intended to do harm, to commit more murders.

It would not be this night.

Not while he was there.

Chapter 39

Little Italy

It was an unexpectedly warm and sunny afternoon for a November. Visitors to Manhattan walked around the city, took in the holiday displays on Fifth Avenue storefronts and explored the many tourist sites and areas listed in all the guide books.

One of them was Little Italy.

Not listed in any guidebook was a four floor apartment building on a side street in Little Italy. Once home to immigrant Italian families, the Drugs for Diamonds crime family often met there.

It had been converted for their modern day use.

The first floor was for meetings and business conferences. The second was divided into half a dozen bedrooms for workers. The third floor had more luxurious surroundings with beautiful mahogany desks and at least half a dozen telephones, all with different numbers. The bosses directed the operation from there.

The fourth floor held the merchandise for Drugs for Diamonds. There was a garage belonging to the building making it possible for merchandise to be delivered late at night, unseen by anyone who valued their life. Neighboring business owners and residents all kept quiet. The, or else, was implied.

The family had operated in secret here for many years. The building held stories and lies about cheating, murders and extensive criminal activities.

Dora heard Donnelly talking about plans for the family to meet in Little Italy. He also mentioned an address they had been watching for quite some time. They should have known she wouldn't think twice of checking it out herself. She was so convinced who the head of the family was she could hardly contain herself. On the taxi ride to Little Italy, she remembered what *he* told her, that famous man, now retired living in the Mansion. "You're impatient."

"Zero, I honestly think he's head of the family. We need some hard evidence. Please, only a couple hours. Let's see if we can find out anything."

"This is crazy. He's well respected."

"I know. That's what makes this so disconcerting. His position and reputation allows him a lot of power."

"And powerful connections." Zero was dressed for sleuthing or a prison break, wearing a cheap black sweatshirt and sweatpants, being true to himself he had on a thousand dollar leather jacket. Black, of course.

Dora, hiding her hair in a knit hat, also dressed all in black, agreed.

They looked more like a couple ready to rob a bank.

"Really, Lady D, I doubt anyone in Little Italy will talk to us even if they know anything. Probably scared to death of them. And, darling, I mean that literally."

"Okay, I said we'll sit here having coffee, and then we can wander through the area casually asking about him."

From the minute they arrived in Little Italy they had been watched.

The crime family boss had a bad feeling the night before. He was an astute and unscrupulous man. When she flinched seeing him, he knew he would soon have to make a move away from the business.

Dora and Zero were under scrutiny everywhere they went.

The family boss told his people, "I want you to destroy them. Her husband too. Get rid of these people."

Blythe called Dick on Monday around noon to tell him what Dora was planning on doing. She felt it was way too dangerous. Soon after, Dick and Donnelly read a similar message from Zero about what they were doing and why.

They were furious.

"Dora and I are in Little Italy. She's pretty sure who the family leader is and you'll be shocked. The two of you need to get down here to save and protect us. I can't get her to leave. Yes, before you even ask, I tried to stop her from coming here. I need your help before we get killed."

Detective Donnelly, Dick and two plainclothes policemen in a separate car arrived in Little Italy as Dora and Zero walked out of the bakery.

Punching Zero, she asked, "You told them?"

"Sweetheart, I figured better for you to be angry at me than them finding us dead in one of the side alleys here."

"We're fine."

"The hell you are," said Donnelly. "Don't you know you've been watched for the past several days? I got a call from Mario, told us you, Dick, Zero and V are to be 'taken care of.' We had plainclothes police at the event last night and outside the Mansion. You're also being followed, so I'm sure you're not fine here."

Pulling them back inside the bakery, they found a table near the back, got more coffee and one of the police officers walked in nodded and walked back out.

"What does that mean?" Dora asked, angry and sarcastic.

"Two more patrol cars I requested just arrived. You're not going anywhere without police protection, especially in this neighborhood."

"Damn it, Dick, why don't you say something?"

"Because, I might kill the two of you myself. And so you know, Blythe also called to let me know what you were up to and who you both saw in those photos."

"Oh." Dora sat back, crossed her arms, and didn't say another word, for the moment.

Zero figured he best be quiet too. At least for the moment anyhow.

"What is he talking about? Who you saw in those photos?" Donnelly was furious at their antics that put all of them in danger.

"I'm pretty sure I know who the head of the family is. I didn't think you would believe me unless I had more proof. Blythe saw the photos and agrees with me."

Slamming his fist on the table, other customers turning to look at him, Detective Donnelly shouted, "Stop this nonsense. Think about it for heaven's sake. Two people murdered in a week, attempts on both your lives. Don't you sit there so smug, Zero, remember, you're on their hit list too."

With that Zero got up, went to the bakery counter and bought the biggest pastry on their shelves and sat down to eat it without a bit of guilt.

At least not for eating the pastry.

Dora reached into her handbag and pulled out the two photos Donnelly had sent to her and set them on the table in front of him and Dick.

"Here, tell me what you see."

After a few minutes of no comments from them, Dora explained what it was that caught her attention.

Donnelly and Dick starred at the photos, looked up at each other, and back at the photos.

"Really? Him?"

"Yes, really."

"He hugged me last night." Zero almost choked on his pastry.

"Yes, he did." Dick found himself smiling.

"The three of you, let's get out of here. If he really is the head of the family the only safe place for you is at the Mansion with police protection. Although I would prefer to put Dora and Zero in jail for a few days."

"Hey, I'm an innocent bystander pushed into bad behavior by this lovely lady."

Dick got up, and pulled Dora to him. She had the good sense to go along quietly, although there was certainly a twinkle in her eye.

"I'll get some more photos of them together. How about I bring them over to you this evening? I'm going to check out a few more things about Mr. Important. You're to stay put, understand!" Donnelly got up and started making calls for warrants.

She watched silently, peering through windows with mostly closed heavy drapes. Same as the ones she remembered seeing in the Martin sisters' condo.

Chapter 40

Dick and Dora

"Once we get the leaders the rest will fall apart."

Donnelly met with officers and other detectives in his Manhattan precinct, instructing the desk sergeant not to let anyone outside of the station know the plans.

"They have eyes and ears all over the city."

Home, safe and sound, police outside their door and downstairs, Dick and Dora sipped on cocktails while the planned capture of the crime family was unfolding.

"I'm going home to change clothes. I'll be up to join you soon." Zero had headed to his place, a guard there as well.

The take down wouldn't happen all at once. Too much money and power was at stake for the family to go quietly.

"Stop being upset with me."

"You know why I'm upset. You could have gotten hurt or worse. And poor Zero dragging him along at your insistence."

"He was happy with his big Italian pastry."

"Dora, none of this is funny."

"Dear, maybe you and your pals should play poker later. Gambling always calms you down. You could have a game here protected by the police."

"Sweetheart, I don't want to be calm. I may stay mad at you for days, maybe months."

Truth was he never could stay mad at her for long at all.

They were expecting Donnelly. "I'll be there about seven. I have more photos and background information on our suspect, thanks to our resident computer geek."

Both Zero and Carson planned to join them. Neither wanted to miss any of the drama unfolding.

Waiting, Dora suddenly got up, with Dick watching her. "Now what?"

She made two phone calls without answering him.

When she was done, he smiled at her.

Dora had called their sons wishing them a belated Happy Thanksgiving. "Wanted to be sure you know we love you guys."

Each son concerned, asked, "Mom are you okay? Is something wrong? Is Dad there?"

This type of call was unusual for Dora, she knew it. Dick knew it.

So did they.

"Yes, darling. We're fine. We miss you. Join us in Vegas. We'll be there in about a week. Bring the family. We'll make reservations at your favorite hotel on the strip."

Half an hour later, hanging up the phone, Dora glanced over at Dick

"Yes, dear, I know, this is quite a mess we're in the middle of—again."

Zero had appeared at their door, knocking loudly. "Hey guys, open up, wait until you hear this."

Behind him was Donnelly with Carson only steps behind both of them.

"Get inside, I told all of you not to go anywhere."

"This isn't anywhere." At the moment cute didn't go over well with Donnelly.

"Wait until they hear what? Someone else get killed?"

"Not killed. Married."

The Zimms had no idea what Zero was talking about.

"I should have taken bets on this happening."

"Damn it, Zero. What's happening to who?"

"Married to each other, that's what."

Dora got up, pulled Zero by the arm and pushed him none too gently onto the sofa. "Who got married to whom?"

"Blinkie and Red."

Donnelly and the Zimms were speechless.

"Seems they've been seeing each other for months. They weren't here for Thanksgiving, not that we noticed, our trying to not get killed."

"Where are they? When did they get married?" Dora demanded to know more.

"Vegas, yesterday."

Dora was speechless. Dick was grinning. Detective Donnelly was also in no mood for romance.

"If all of you will set wedded bliss aside, check out these photos."

Donnelly set six photos on their dining room table.

"The way he's got a hold of her, it's the same in all the photos. It's what I told Blythe, when I was a judge in divorce court and an attorney brought in photos of a spouse who had been abused. Similar body language."

"We've spent the afternoon checking on Grant Richardson. His cell phone records show frequent calls to Brooklyn and Little Italy. His bank records reveal a convoluted system of personal and business accounts in a dozen countries. He's worth millions. We couldn't access many pieces, there are layers upon layers."

"You think he's the crime family boss?" Dick stood up, pacing, asking what needed to be asked.

"I do."

"Told you so." Dora smugly sat back on one of her dining room chairs. "Now what?"

"We're getting a search warrant for the building in Little Italy and the house in Brooklyn. We want to have an element of surprise so we're going in at midnight tonight. Judge gave me a hell of a time about the search warrants but we had enough compelling evidence, so he finally relented. Said if I'm wrong to look for a new job."

"You're right." Dora looked up at him.

"I better be. I'm too old to change careers. All hell is going to break loose over his arrest."

Answering his phone, Donnelly grabbed the photos. “Probably worse. I gotta go, we just got the search warrants.”

“Notify Carson. He deserves to have an inside edge on the story.”

Donnelly replied as he rushed out, “Done already.”

At one A.M. Donnelly called Dick. “The head of the family and Blanche can’t be found.”

Chapter 41

Juice in the Game

Former Governor Grant Richardson had been retired from public office for over twenty years. A reputation for being a rainmaker, he could help others succeed as he did.

But at what price?

Dora, restless and increasingly anxious since Richardson and Martin were missing, went on her own internet search about them, especially Richardson.

"Dick, listen to what was written about Richardson a few years ago: 'Grant Richardson has what is known as 'juice in the game,' a genius at understanding the political and business worlds. He has influential friends in New York, D.C. and other centers of power.'"

"Read on, Macbeth."

"It goes on to say 'He's also a master of manipulation and control, often demanding business deals be completed in terms he wants. His reputation for filing bankruptcy in order to not pay people who did the work for him is legendary.'"

"A true egomaniac. What about personal?"

"Married over forty years to the same woman, no children, and an apartment in Manhattan's Upper East Side. Darling, listen to this, 'for years there has been unsubstantiated gossip that he was born to an Italian woman in Brooklyn who died years ago.'"

"What does he say?"

"It says he always responds with one word. 'Ridiculous.'"

"Certainly would connect him from birth to the family."

"Dick, here's an anonymous response to the article. 'Grant Richardson is clever and arrogant. He often bullies people who work for him. No one dares complain. In whispered corners of government his reputation is one of beware, don't make him angry.'"

"I'm surprised the paper published that without being sued."

"Maybe they were, doesn't say anything about that here. The discoveries about him were, well and still are, remarkable…and awful. Love, I could use a drink."

Dick got up, glad to oblige.

When Carson had been there earlier he gave them some of the background information he recently uncovered in files marked private and confidential. Most of it however came from private interviews he managed to get with Mario Russo. He had been like a dog with a bone determined to know the whole story, and what better source than Cutter's son falsely imprisoned and angry over the murder of his brother Vincent.

According to Mario "The depths of Richardson's dark side were fueled by his being groomed since youth to be head of the crime family. The always un-named Italian woman had given birth to him and his brother, Cutter."

Carson had asked Mario, "We know Cutter was born Christian Russo. How did Grant Richardson get his name?"

"Several times over the years I heard the family paid a couple in upstate New York to adopt him when he was around seven years old and give him their name so there would be no outward connection to any of us."

"Do you know what happened to those people?"

"No, and I never saw or met them. They could be dead for all I know. Good chance they killed them to keep them quiet."

"Was Cutter mad that Grant eventually became head of the family?"

"Nah. It had always been assumed Cutter started the gang and mob warfare when in fact it had been started years earlier by his father and his buddies. Although it was taken over by an overly aggressive and clearly pathological Cutter, it was always assumed his brother would eventually take over. He was much smarter, even Cutter accepted the family decision. Grant's name was not mentioned, only as his brother."

"So how did they hide him and groom him?" Dora was clearly fascinated as Carson continued telling her and Dick the details he got from Mario Russo.

"According to Mario it was obvious to everyone he was exceptionally bright. He was sent to private school, college and law school. A couple of judges and some police in the family helped with the legalities. After graduating with honors from law school, the plan to get him elected governor began to take shape. The contacts he made in college gave him access to people with money and power. Every summer growing up through law school, Grant Richardson spent on a farm in upstate New York with members of the family grooming him for his future."

Dick was getting restless. Dora knew he was more than ready to get to Las Vegas away from this mess but Carson continued.

"Mario recalled hearing people talking about Richardson. He said, 'I was younger so they didn't pay me much attention, but I listened, pretending I was reading or watching television so they ignored me.'"

"What were they telling him?"

"We need you to play the game well. Deceive others. Never let anyone know your true identity. Your role as head of the family has major demands and implications for all of us and our business."

The crime family story was growing deeper and darker, the more everyone involved in solving this case knew, the more complex and complicated it appeared to be.

Diamonds, drugs, murders, deceit, and secret lives. Donnelly had told them even more. "The rich and powerful thought he was one of them, supporting his venture into politics, first as a state senator for two terms, then governor. They gave him power. He gave them access to that power. His learned and practiced outward demeanor could easily switch from generous philanthropist to hand shaking politician to violence against anyone he considered an enemy."

"I recall some stories about him," Dick commented.

"Regular editorials by him appeared in New York papers when he was in office, complaining, blaming or accusing someone he believed was against him or his policies. He had powerful enemies who disliked and distrusted him. In response to his rants they sent out emails to the paper and hundreds of their own contacts."

"He's nuts."

"The man is definitely crazy."

"Psychotic."

"A fool."

"A dangerous fool."

"Unbelievable that no one had any idea who he really was," Dora remarked quietly.

"Richardson was very clever, he never responded to those comments. His role as head of the biggest crime family on the east coast demanded ignoring such remarks. Once out of office, his letters to the editor ceased. He kept his powerful contacts and easily became part of the establishment to the outside world."

"Obviously he secretly continued to be head of the family." Dick stood up to get a drink, growing more concerned about their safety.

"His rants were confined to anyone in the family he believed had messed up. Depending on the situation some were beaten, others murdered. The many bodies in the meatpacking plant are proof of that. The details and evidence coming out will keep the police busy for one hell of a long time."

Donnelly sounded more than a little frustrated and concerned.

The public didn't get to see the Grant Richardson who had grown up to be a monster.

Chapter 42

The Blue Light

"They're gone?"

"Where?"

"Drove out of their apartment building garage in Little Italy into the dark even before we knocked on the door."

"Anyone know where they are?"

"Not that anyone is saying."

"We're increasing police presence at the Mansion."

"Zero is here, invited himself in for a drink couple hours ago."

"Tell him to stay put. I assume he knows about the search warrants?"

"Sure, we've been waiting to hear from you or Carson."

Donnelly was on his cell phone with Dick, the call meant to warn them.

"Dick, these two are most likely planning on killing you and Dora. Zero would be a bonus."

Poor Zero.

After hearing all this from Dick, he slumped down on the sofa and turned on the television. Perfect. There was an old Abbott and Costello film showing them being chased by bad guys.

Dick went out on the small balcony, facing the avenue and the diner across the street where Socks often hung out. Quickly turning on an outdoor blue light bulb, he came back inside to wait.

There was nothing else to do but wait. For now.

Within fifteen minutes the avenue in front of the Mansion was closed with half a dozen police cars, an ambulance and a fire truck posted in front, all with flashing lights.

"Good grief, they're ready for Armageddon," shouted Zero.

Dora pushed Zero's feet off the sofa and sat down to watch the silly film with him. "Darling, is someone knocking?"

"Can't be, there's a police officer standing guard. We're being protected by the finest."

Dick's attempt at lightheartedness was going nowhere. He heard the knock too, then a tiny voice.

"Dick, Dora, its Bertie Gladstone, open up. What's going on?"

Concerned for her and their police protection, he opened the door to pull her inside.

They were waiting!

The police officer had been shot, the sound muffled by a silencer.

They were waiting in the dark stairway for the right moment to go in with their demands. Demands to help them get out of the country.

Bertie coming to the Zimmerman's door was the perfect moment.

Grant Richardson and Blanche Martin pushed Bertie inside and locked the door behind them, guns pointed at the four people in the apartment.

Dora was helping Bertie up from the floor. Luckily only her ego was bruised.

"Bertie why are you here?"

"I saw flashing lights below from my bedroom window."

"Shut up, all of you, and sit down. You're going to do exactly as I tell you." Richardson was talking. Blanche was silent, sporting a shiner.

"Call your detective. Tell him we're here and we want a plane to take us out of the country."

"Somewhere where there is no extradition, I presume. Joining the traitor Snowden?"

"Get him on the phone or I'll begin shooting. You can be sure it will be your wife first."

"How the hell did he get there?" Donnelly shouted over the phone.

"He is demanding to speak to you."

"Detective Donnelly, you better listen to me. The people you're concerned about are with us. Meaning Dick, Dora, Zero and for some reason Carson's grandmother is here."

Negotiations went back and forth, with Donnelly agreeing to the demands telling Richardson it would take a few hours.

"You have two hours to make it happen or everyone here is dead."

Dora had her arm around Bertie. "Why did you come here?"

"Figured you two would know what's happening. I'm always up around this time. Did you know that between midnight and two A.M. is huge for home shopping networks?"

"What are you talking about?"

"Old people. I'm talking about old people."

"Why old people?"

"Dora, most old people eat dinner at four, are in bed by seven and are wide awake walking around again anytime from midnight to two A.M. Television shopping is a big hit at that hour. For me it's like window-shopping."

"Be quiet, you two, and turn off the television."

"I am curious, may I ask, how you got inside the building?"

Dick was talking slowly, softly. He knew they needed as much time as possible for the police to resolve this situation.

He knew he had some safeguards in place, hoping they would work. He wanted to keep Richardson engaged in conversation.

Grinning, he said, "You're all fools. We got into the Mansion's side door with Blanche's key and of course she had the alarm code. None of you idiots thought to change it."

"From there?" Dick acted as if he was impressed.

"We took the elevator to the tenth floor and walked the next two flights, not wanting anyone to hear the elevator open up on the penthouse floor. I shot the policeman before he could even pull out his gun and dragged him into the stairwell to hide him."

"How long were you waiting there?"

"Not very long. This fancy old lady didn't realize anyone else was up here."

"I would have hit you with my walker if I did."

"Bertie," Dora said, taking her hand. "Let's all sit here quietly."

Pulling her purse next to her, Bertie sat on the sofa close to Dora.

"All of you, sit down. We either get out of here or this place will look like a version of The Saint Valentine's Day massacre."

Donnelly was desperate knowing Richardson was serious about his threat, trying to figure out how to get to him.

"Detective, I need to talk to you."

"Not now."

"Yes now." Frankie Socks came over to him to tell him about the blue light on the Zimms' patio.

"Dick puts the blue light on when he needs help."

"We know he needs help. Any bright ideas?"

"The light also means he left his bedroom window by the fire escape unlocked and opened slightly. I'm sure he wants me to tell you."

"I'm sure he does. We got this, thanks."

Detective Donnelly went over to two of his officers wearing bulletproof vests and told them about the fire escape and window and within minutes the three of them started the climb.

Most of the floors were dark. The Mansion residents were either asleep or pretending to be. This was not a night for them to do anything else.

Knowing the threats against him and Dora were serious, Dick told Socks about his blue light idea. Socks agreed to spend more time at his favorite diner so he could keep a watch on the Mansion.

"How did you know the police were after you tonight?" Dora glanced over at Richardson.

"I knew trouble was coming soon. I saw the way you looked at me the other night and figured you realized who I was. Smart cookie, your wife," he said to Dick. "Let's hope it doesn't get you all killed."

"What about the search warrants? Did you know about them?" Dick was still talking slowly, cautiously.

"All these years, you don't think I have safety measures in place? The doorman at my apartment building works for me, you fool. He texted my wife and she texted me. All in minutes of the search warrant being granted."

"Someone on the take inside the police station?"

"More than one someone. Power demands little people take orders."

"Is Blanche one of the little people? She has quite a black eye. Bet it hurts."

Dick wanted to keep him talking. He was sure Socks would know what to tell Donnelly about the blue light.

"Blanche made a mistake. She had to pay for it. She understands that."

Blanche, looking like she really wanted to kill someone, hadn't said a word since they pushed their way into the Zimms' condo.

Neither had Zero. As a betting man, he knew the odds of getting killed were pretty good if he started acting like a smart aleck.

He was also watching Bertie talking to Dora, desperately trying to show her something in the bright red cloth purse she always carried.

Dora was shaking her head no ever so slightly, glancing quickly up at Dick, both feeling a bit helpless at the moment.

Donnelly called, "There's a limo in front of the building that will take you to a private airfield at Kennedy Airport. The plane will be ready within the hour."

"Get the limo to the back of the building. It's darker and I don't want funny moves from any of you. We'll be holding a gun on your pals."

"I'll call you back as soon as we get all this in place."

"Do it now!"

Desperately attempting to not sound out of breath from making the climb, Donnelly hung up and then had one of the officers signal the police below they had reached the twelfth floor where the Zimms lived.

To some it seemed a ridiculous expense to have fire escapes on this building. Many who lived in Manhattan on September 11th didn't think so.

Helicopters were flying over the area, bright lights below. Donnelly was furious. If this was shown on television, everyone inside the Zimmerman's home would be killed. A full moon over a sky of winter clouds moving quickly added to the insane drama of the night.

When the Mansion fire alarm suddenly went off, the piercing sound brought residents, some annoyed, some frightened, into the halls. A police officer on each floor refused to answer questions, instead instructing them to go back inside their homes.

None of them needed to know what was happening.

The noise of the alarm was intended to block out the sound of the bedroom window opening and three police officers climbing inside. The tension in the living room became worse when the apartment went dark and only holiday lights from outside gave any light inside.

"Sometimes when there's a fire, electricity goes out." Dick was doing his best to sound convincing, moving closer to Dora and Bertie. That's when he saw the darling eighty-nine year old Bertie, sitting very close to Dora, had a gun in her purse.

Zero saw Dick tell her to put her purse down next to him.

Richardson was screaming, "We're through waiting. We've waited long enough."

It was exactly enough.

The police rushed into the living room, Dick pulled out Bertie's gun and Zero rushed next to Dora and Bertie pushing them onto the floor.

Richardson punched one of the police officers, Blanche kicked and cursed another officer and Dick shot Richardson, who collapsed on the floor. Blanche was screaming at everyone as Dora got up and hit her on the head with a sculpture of *The Thinker*.

It became quite a topic of discussion later on.

After several more minutes of upheaval the two were handcuffed and taken out of the condo to a police escort, Richardson limping because Dick had hit him in the leg. Blanche, her head bleeding, was still kicking and screaming.

"Nice shooting, Law Man."

"Very funny."

"You have Frankie Socks to thank for our saving your behinds."

"My brilliant idea."

"That it was, my friend. That it was."

"They sure can curse a lot." Dora hugged her husband, then Bertie.

Zero started laughing so hard, they didn't know what was wrong with him.

"Dora hits Blanche with *The Thinker* and Bertie carries a gun? You don't find all that all this is too funny for words?"

Chapter 43

Drugs for Diamonds

The Wall Street money people who loved their drugs didn't give a damn how they got them. They paid the family for them in diamonds, never in cash.

"That's why I think expanding to the Miami area would be a success. It's surrounded by wealthy communities like Jupiter and West Palm."

Blanche had continued to be outspoken about her support for expanding there.

In planning their expansion, the head of the family stressed, "The desire and demand for drugs is not going away. In addition to all those wealthy buyers, drugs are being sold to college students, housewives and soccer moms, by other drug users, so they have money to feed their own drug habit."

The family didn't care where the diamond payments came from. Many were stolen from family heirlooms, wives' jewelry, jewelry stores and resources from wholesalers around the world. The wealthy had connections. In addition to spending millions in diamonds to pay for their drug habit they were thieves.

The diamonds were usually re-cut and sold to an international client list that included major department stores, private buyers and even some of the larger jewelry stores. They easily turned a blind eye to what they were buying. It meant more money for them.

The family sold diamonds for huge amounts of money. Money with which they paid the drug lords. Full circle, those who used the drugs purchased them from the family with diamonds.

Trusted connections from India, Columbia and even a few drug lords in the United States kept them supplied. Transition to Drugs for Diamonds years earlier, from prostitution and drug trafficking was easy since the drug lords and the crime family made a fortune.

Detective Donnelly revealed the whole convoluted business scheme to the Zimms, Zero and Carson.

"Grant Richardson knew how to wheel and deal, to make money, lots of money. The family had secure bank accounts and private investment holdings in half a dozen countries. He also made sure his drug contacts were kept happy. 'They like money, booze and women,' he told the family more than once."

Donnelly continued, "The family had little, if any scruples. They willingly kept the people they bought drugs from happy. 'Be sure they have plenty of all three.' That was Richardson's motto."

"True capitalism," Dick laughed.

"Very much so. Their whole house of cards was discovered after we seized their bank accounts and bookkeeping records from Richardson's home. Shows years of earning millions."

"Does that mean I should check my jewels?" Dora put her arm around Dick, grinning.

"Darling, I gave them all to Bertie. You know she's my secret love."

Donnelly interrupted the banter. "By the way, Tess Martin also wrote in her diary that she stuffed the diamonds into Alphonse's throat. She wanted to make a statement that he was a thief and con man."

"Certifiable," announced Zero standing behind them, taking bets on his phone about the head of the family.

"He'll get life."

"I bet he'll kill himself in jail."

"Someone will murder him before he gets sentenced."

It went on like that for several days until Zero shut down the betting, and announced, "I need to pack my bikini and head west."

"We are going to Vegas. Soon," declared Dick.

Dora and Zero both said a very loud, YES.

Cut and uncut diamonds were found on the fourth floor of the apartment building in Little Italy. Along with dozens of purchase orders from stores around the world buying them in a type of black market arrangement set up by the crime family. It was brilliant.

The house in Brooklyn revealed documents found in a safe listing all the contacts for buying the drugs, clients who purchased diamonds with drugs and more family secrets.

It would take months for the police to review everything and have a complete picture of the family's enterprise.

Carson Gladstone once again had what he needed to write his next story. "The description of the knife, photos, surveillance tape, the gun used for the attempted murder of Dick Zimmerman, DNA found near Vincent's body, a hit man in jail for going after V, not to mention attempts to kill Dora and Zero in Little Italy and the final showdown at the Zimms' apartment. They had the Drugs for Diamonds crime family dead to rights."

According to Carson's article, "Grant Richardson, the former governor, is accused of being behind the murder of dozens of people, illegal drug activities and money laundering. Blanche Martin and Gina Torelli are accused of being accomplices in the criminal enterprise, including the recent murders of Alphonse Romero, Vincent Blair and Tess Martin."

Donnelly told them, "There was hope for V and Mario. Once he was released from prison, they would be put into the Witness Protection Program."

Grant Richardson, while awaiting trial, was stabbed to death in prison by an unknown assailant. There were plenty of inmates with a reason to want the man dead.

No one was going to snitch on who killed him.

Donnelly reminded them, “It had been well known that Governor Richardson had pushed for the death penalty, and treated people on his staff with disdain, bordering on cruelty (according to sources). Some abandoned their careers in the political world to escape his irrational and illogical behavior.”

One unidentified staff member was quoted in a state political newspaper, “He is an out of control narcissist who has no idea how to govern. He’s paranoid and almost pathological in his behavior.”

“Okay, so, there were a lot of people who had it out for the man. What about his wife?” Dora was ready for this to all be over.

“Let me finish, then you can get on your way out of here and I can hope that you won’t be involved in any murders when you’re back here.”

“Any bets on that detective?” Zero wasn’t as funny as he thought he was. At least not to Detective Donnelly.

“Richardson’s wife was also arrested. Her name and signature are on numerous documents and bank accounts. She was not the shrinking violet she pretended to be. Their Manhattan apartment will filled with expensive furniture and antiques and a private art collection worth a fortune according to papers we found. They agreed to the marriage as a front for their business empire and to make him desirable as a politician. Hidden documents outlined their financial arrangement. It was all for show.”

The media, especially Carson Gladstone had a field day for weeks writing about the ever-evolving story.

Carson continued to gather information for a tell-all book on what he was calling the crime family of the century. Everyone in the crime family was refused bail. Their crimes, over many years, horrendous and egregious.

When asked, Zero refused to say who won the bet about Grant Richardson.

"Of course there are still bets on the two of you and your being crime fighters."

Dora gave him a dirty look. Dick said nothing. Zero laughed out loud. He knew the two of them couldn't stay out of trouble.

Chapter 44

It Is You

He opened the door to Zero, asking in an almost sheepish manner, “Could we talk? I know you’ve spoken to Dick and Dora.”

“I would like that. I’ve noticed you.”

“Really?”

“You interest me.”

“Why?”

“Your humor is reflected in how you dress.”

“So?”

“It’s all quite an act, isn’t it?”

Zero laughed so hard, he bent over, his arms wrapped around himself almost falling off the straight back chair he was sitting on.

“You mean like the orange t-shirt I’m wearing? Says, *I’m hot* on the front. *You’re not* on the back.”

“Yes, like that.”

“Makes me feel young. Playful. I don’t like feeling old.”

“I don’t mind being old. Brings wisdom, if you allow it.”

"Have you gained wisdom over the years?"

"I like to think so."

"You've had an incredible life."

"I did. I bet, no pun intended, you did too."

"Perhaps."

"I heard you received a wonderful honor the other night?"

"I did. They certainly surprised me."

"It must tell you how highly people think of you. How much the good you've done for others is appreciated."

"True."

"You have delightful friends like Dick and Dora."

"I do. Funny, I find we're good at letting small bits of bad in our lives take over the huge amount of good."

"It's a common fault of humanity."

"Amongst many other faults."

"Of course."

Zero stretched out his legs, looking over at the years of the man's career in photos, same as Dick and Dora had recently done.

"Do you miss the work?"

"Sometimes. I miss friends I made. Many of them gone."

"Another common fault of life."

"Not our choice. Happens when it happens."

"Except when people are murdered."

"Yes that does eliminate choice."

"Someone tried to murder us recently, quite a raucous event."

"I heard. Gossip mill here is in full fervor, including on the elevator."

"For sure. Did you ever meet the head of our gossip gang, Bertie Gladstone?"

"Oh yes, we've met several times. She comes sauntering up to me, smiling, telling me she thinks she's seen me before."

"She is a charmer, must have been some looker in her younger days."

"Probably. I smile back and tell her I have a common face."

"She was a big help when we were all being threatened."

"Did she hit them with her walker?"

"I swear to you, that cute little old lady was carrying a gun in her purse."

"Good to know. Good to know. I'll be careful around her."

Finishing a fine bottle of wine, heavy snowflakes were flattening themselves against his living room windows.

"Why not call the Zimmerman's to join us?"

"Lovely idea." Zero grinning at this famous man sitting in a century old rocking chair sighed. He knew this man would be his friend.

"Delighted to see you both again."

"We've brought some liquid refreshment."

"Good, we've finished our bottle of wine."

Dick popped the champagne, pouring some into deep blue flutes he'd brought with them. "To friends. And to warm weather."

"I assume you've been wanting to hear about my life as a film star in the 40's and 50's. Perhaps I should tell you a little about it."

They smiled, nodding yes. Dick would get up a couple times to refill their champagne glasses, then sit next to Dora, her legs folded under her like a child listening to a bedtime story.

"Those films and many of their directors had a major influence on the industry and because of some of them, mystery stories became increasingly popular. Noir films, always in black and white, set a mood with the place and the people. Stories were usually in big cities, dark places, dim lighting, sometimes bad weather and lots of shadows cast on walls and stairways."

"Hmm, sounds like the meatpacking plant," Dick commented.

"I read that article. I would say exactly like that. You could feel its evil and darkness. The sense of mystery and crime, the confusion it caused, all quite similar to films I appeared in."

"What about romantic scenes?" Dora grinned.

"Of course, there were romantic scenes and many of the films had great lighthearted moments with funny one-liners."

"Did you ever direct any of them?"

"No, I was content to act in them. Made me a star and a lot of money."

"Any favorites?"

"Probably, but I'm not going to tell you which ones. You can decide which you like best. They're replayed often on television."

"Most of my characters had a combination of charm and an edge to them. Sort of like the three of you."

"You think we're characters?" Dick was smiling at his host.

"My young man, who of course compared to me you are young, you and your wife should have a movie made of your antics. Add Zero to the characters and you'll have one heck of a delightful film."

"Nah, we're retired."

"Sure you are. And I'm a teen idol."

"You're still a famous film star idol thanks to old movies on television."

"Let's finish the champagne. Remember, I know people in the film business. I've already decided I am going to present them with a storyline about Dick and Dora Zimmerman and their sidekick, Zero the bookie."

"Would you act in it?"

"Good heavens no. Maybe a cameo would be fun, like Hitchcock used to do."

"You better change the names to protect the innocent, or anyone else for that matter." Dick laughed as Dora uncurled herself from the sofa to go over and give him a kiss on the cheek.

"Now I'm the envy of millions of film noir enthusiasts."

"More would be envious of me being kissed by you, my dear."

Another hour of delightful, fun conversation and champagne ended the evening with their neighbor and new friend.

Dick later called it fascinating, Dora remarking, he's amazing. "I wish Greta Garbo could play me in the movie."

"What about Clark Gable for me?"

They would go on like that for days.

Memories of him, of their own lives.

Zero last to leave, told the film legend as he closed the door, "Not to worry, I won't tell Bertie it's you."

A familiar movie star voice was left laughing.

Chapter 45

Back Table at Mickey's

Rehashing the story of the crime family activities, the extent of their being serial murderers, their capture and Bertie's gun had Zero embellishing how he nearly got killed.

They were only connected by a series of strange events beginning with the Martin sisters bumping into Dick at the elevator. Everyone agreed it was his fault they were involved.

Dick stood up. "I protest. Bring me more drink."

"Sit down, darling."

Joined only by Donnelly and Mickey, Socks preferring his diner, and Carson working late on another story. It had been almost a week since Zero was honored and less than a week since the crime family caper had ended with the arrests.

There would be much more to the story when they appeared in court.

Former Governor Grant Richardson's arrest shocked the country.

"These are lies by my enemies who want to smear my good name."

It wouldn't matter. Beginning with the murder of Alphonse Romero, he and the rest of the family had taken a path toward destruction based on arrogance and greed.

Their entitlement was extreme hubris, believing they could do anything they wanted and get away with it. They threatened to sue and get even some day.

They lost their voices and their power. It was over for them.

There would be years of trials and imprisonment, decisions to be made on what to do with the millions of dollars of diamonds found in the Little Italy building and dealing with a few disgruntled drug lords who had expected those diamonds as payment for drugs they provided the family.

"Not exactly something you can go to the police for," Detective Donnelly said, sitting back, a pleased man.

"Couldn't happen to a nicer bunch of crooks. Here's to you senior sleuths." Mickey toasted them and placed a bottle of expensive wine on the table.

"Thank you, my good man." Dick preferred gambling to drinking but this night they had much cause to feel good.

Zero was wearing a bright yellow parka coat. Dick told him he looked like a big bumblebee.

"It is time for us to go to Vegas for a few months to warm up. There I shall shed this coat for my leopard bikini swim suit."

Snow had been falling steady for several days.

"Are Blinkie and Red there?" Dick was still amused at their getting married.

"Blinkie always professed he would never get remarried, too many women would be sad if he did, and Red once claimed, 'I prefer cute little puppies, they give great kisses.'"

Dora sat down her glass, and took a piece of paper out of her jacket pocket. "Ahem, I shall read this message from them. 'Dear friends and loved ones, we are having our honeymoon in Vegas, weather is great, wine is chilled and well, we are…'"

Everyone laughed, they got the idea.

EPILOGUE

Senior Sleuthing Promises

Dora had announced at Mickey's, "My husband and I have promised each other no more sleuthing."

The poker-playing cronies had a bet with Zero.

"They'll get involved in more murders."

Zero had begun his drive from Manhattan to Las Vegas. They had all heard his declaration of travel before. "I don't fly."

"You're a wimp, my friend."

Dick and Dora smiled. They knew why.

Sitting in first class seats flying to Vegas, two hours into the flight, Dora shook Dick awake. "Darling, there's something wrong with the man sitting across from you. He hasn't moved or touched his food."

"Probably sleeping."

"I don't think so, dear. He looks dead to me."

He was.

About the Author

Marcia Rosen has previously published four books in her mystery series, "Dying to Be Beautiful." Rosen is also author of "The Woman's Business Therapist" and "My Memoir Workbook. " She was founder and owner of a successful Marketing and Public Relations Agency for many years and received numerous awards for her work with business and professional women. She currently resides in Carmel, California.

For more information, visit www.theseniorsleuths

Marcia G. Rosen, member of:

Sisters In Crime, Los Angeles and National

Private Eye Writers
Public Safety Writers Association
Central Coast Writers
Greater Los Angeles Writers Society
Woman's National Book Association.
PULSE, New York

Acknowledgements

My sincere appreciation to Level Best Books for a wonderful working relationship.

68106243R00156

Made in the USA
San Bernardino, CA
31 January 2018